AF260934

This book is a work of fiction. Names, places, events and characters are fictitious in every regard. Any similarity to actual events or persons, living or dead, is purely coincidental.

Butt Boys: Gay Anal Erotica
Copyright©2014 Barry Lowe
ISBN 978-1-909934-64-1
Cover art and design by Dawné Dominique

Published by
Lydian Press 2014
Find us on the World Wide Web at
www.lydianpress.com

CONTENTS

* Previously published in eBook format by loveyoudivine Alterotica

† Previously published in eBook format by Lydian Press

BUTT BOYS

GAY ANAL EROTICA

Barry Lowe

Lydian Press

Sex, drugs, and insatiable bottoms.

TUNNEL VISION

I'm such a fuckwit. How else would you explain my predicament? The facts speak for themselves; it's two o'clock in the morning, it's the middle of winter, and I'm pissed off my brain – at least I think I'm pissed because it could be drugs wearing nothing but a T-shirt, and jeans, with bare feet. I lost my sneakers somewhere during the night. Where am I? Your guess is as good as mine. Godknowswhereville, attempting to hitch a ride outa here. The whole thing is my own fault. There, I freely admit it. Are you laughing yet?

Why are gay men so fuckin' boring? They'd rather sit around discussing the latest Lady Gaga clip or gay rights for Antarctic penguins than get down to the nitty gritty. Where are the real men? Gay guys who like it rough and ready at the click of their fingers, who want nothing better than to ram a moderately hot just-past-twink-years bottom like me?

I spent the night bored off my brain at a gay pub where a group of gay swingers thought they were on to a good thing by inviting me on a date. Better that they had just thrown me on the ground and had their way with me. A fuckin' date! Do I look like someone who wants to go on a date? Fuck me. My filthy mouth always gets me into trouble. I'm too direct. There, I managed to restrain myself. I was gonna put the F word before at least three or four more of those words in those couple of sentences but I've learned too much of a foul mouth and you sound like one of those wussy porn movies where the actors sprout bad dialogue while looking as bored as I'd felt all fuckin' night. After the pub almost sent me catatonic I headed to a disco where the music almost burst my ear drums and the only action in the Men's was of the snorting or injecting kind and I don't mean injecting in my ass.

It was even an off-night at my favorite leather sex-on-premises venue. It was water sports night. Maybe the idea of a bit of piss turned off the customers because they were conspicuous by their absence. I spent half an hour down on my knees in the prayer position, my jeans soaking up a puddle, wondering whether I'd end up with crippling arthritis in my joints like my old mom, because there was fuck all else going on.

Somewhere between when I'd paid to go into the disco and leaving the leather den, I lost my wallet – or else it'd been lifted by some skanky fag – and I no longer had taxi fare home. Proof enough that I must have been in a bad way, it took me some time to realize I'd left my shoes inside the leather den but when I went back the door was closed and no amount of banging got me an answer. Plus for the first fuckin' time in living memory the weather bureau got it right and the cold front had moved in: a bitterly cold wind that froze my balls off. Only thing in its favor was it made my nipples hard as icicles. Problem was, no one was sucking.

My lack of mates, the sort who'd allow me to sleep on their living room floor let alone share their bed, sank any chance of a warm place to kip. I guess I must have looked the worse for wear because guys were giving me a wide berth as I walked up the street. In frustration, I shouted at one pissy bunch who giggled like high school girls at the fact I had no shoes. "Have I got two fuckin' heads or something?"

No cash for a cab meant sleeping in a park or a shop doorway for the night. I glanced up at the clock on top of the gay pub on the corner. Shit! If I hurried, I might just make the subway. Last train was due to leave in about fifteen minutes. I'd have to jump the turnstiles but that wouldn't be the first time.

I ran down the pavement hoping to make it in time, barging a path through groups of gay men who scrambled to get out of the way of the madman. The underground station loomed and I still had five minutes. My joy was cut short when I noticed the automatic entrance shutter was about two thirds down and closing fast. Bastards. I slid under it on my belly dirtying my fifty-dollar boutique T-shirt. Flinging myself down the escalator because I heard the train pulling into the platform, I managed to wedge myself between the closing doors of the train, scraping my arm against the hard rubber seal but that was the least of my worries.

The carriage was all but empty, a few stragglers like me curled up asleep on the seats, their heads rested against the graffiti-carved windows. Wrapping my arms around my cold torso and propping my feet up under my body, I managed to warm up a little. Big mistake. I had only a few stops to go; a quick twenty minutes on the train but too far to walk on a cold night when I was next to naked. I leaned my head against the window, wondering where I could find me a man with the requisite attitude to fuck me into the ground. I nodded off dreaming of hairy chests, massive thighs and biceps of steel.

I was just about to be taken by a mob of horny bears (the human variety), my cock hard as iron, my asshole quivering with anticipation…

"Hey, mate, wake up. End of the line."

I came to, slowly. My head was fuzzy, my limbs cramped, one of my feet gone to sleep. Where had all those yummy bears gone?

Instead of a hairy bear, I was confronted by a scruffy overweight train guard who didn't look like anyone had sucked his dick in about fifty years, and I wasn't about to alleviate the drought. The sour look on his face revealed he thought I was a troublemaker and he wasn't about to put up with any shit.

"Where are we?" I croaked, swallowing in order to lubricate my dry throat.

"End of the line, mate. Time to get out."

"What time are you headed back?" I asked, thinking I could remain in the carriage for the return journey.

"We ain't. We're going to the car shed next. Come on, hop it."

I unfolded my body, limping to the carriage door, my foot a prickle of pins and needles. As I alighted onto the platform, the bastard blew his whistle close to my ear, and yelled, "Righto, Tom, take her out."

The automatic doors closed and the train took off into the tunnel. I watched it go, wondering which subway station I'd ended at. When I saw the station name stenciled into the old aluminum seat bolted to the tiled wall, I swore under my breath. Shit! It was one of the least patronized on the outer city loop that surfaced in an industrial area used mostly by factory workers Monday through Friday. I trudged up the stairs, the escalators long since turned off, the ticket office closed, out into a suburb that had the appearance of a film noir landscape at night. The main road which ran past the gaping maw of the subway entrance was wet with the drizzle that had begun while I was asleep on the train.

I was so far off the beaten track there was little prospect of a passing car, and any that did was likely to be driven by a serial killer looking for somewhere to torture or dump the body in the boot, or else drug dealers on their way to the meth factory. I had no choice but to stick out my thumb in hope if not expectation of a lift. Fifteen minutes later, when not a solitary vehicle had passed by and hypothermia was beginning to set in, I pulled my thumb back, burying it in the warmth of my jeans pocket.

Fortunately, the shutter to the station was off its track, obviously the result of some expert vandalism, for which I was grateful. It meant I could at least be snug, if not warm, down on the platform.

The station was in darkness, my way badly marked out by the eerie colored illumination from a vending machine that clunked when the cooling mechanism came to life. I was careful making my way down the long flight of stairs, not wanting to tumble to the bottom with a mass of broken bones. When I reached the platform I was surprised to find the lights were dimmed but still on. Unusual, subway platforms were usually darker than a Blitz blackout in order to save on power. I was very grateful someone had forgotten.

Even in subdued light, the station was a scary place to be. I heard phantom trains off in the distance and more than once I looked into the tunnel at either end expecting a train to trundle into view. Way down the line, probably miles from where I was making myself comfortable on the bench along the wall, the wind occasionally made one of those blood-curdling sounds that children are prone to make in imitation of ghosts. I'd hoped to find a discarded newspaper, something to keep me warm, but no such luck. Still, wrapping my arms around my upper body and pulling my feet into the legs of my jeans like a tortoise withdraws its head made me feel less chilly as well as much more secure.

I fell asleep to the sound of metal striking against the tracks, and smiled at the idea of a railway operatic anvil chorus. I woke up to the sound of an explosive clang of heavy metal right near my head. I opened my eyes and blinked, my head throbbing with the reverberations of the noise and the blow against the bench on which I was asleep. I gasped. Standing over me was a giant with a sledge hammer in his hands as if he was about to smack me in the head.

Adrenalin racing through my body I sat up. "Fuck!"

It took a few seconds for my heart rate to calm down and for my eyes to adjust from sleep to the dimly-lit platform and even longer for my brain to catch up with the rest of me. In that time the guy who was tall, but no giant, as I could now assess, ran his eyes from my face down my body. His face lit up.

"Been out partying?" he asked. "Fell asleep on the train?"

I was suddenly cold. "Happen a lot, does it?"

"You'd be surprised what washes up at the end of the line on a weekend." The smile never left his face. He was good-looking in a rough sort of way, wearing a fluoro vest loosely, revealing a body filthy with grime and dirt, jeans that were almost as dirty, and reinforced boots – the sort that working men favor. His arms were thick with muscle, probably from heaving the solid looking hammer he now carried easily over his shoulder.

For some reason known only to the inner recesses of my brain, I decided to go with sarcasm. "So, what are you? Serial killer? Fag basher? Action star? Slumming male model?"

His hearty laugh echoed along the deserted platform. "You think I'm male model material, eh?"

His question gave me the opportunity to ogle him more openly from top to bottom than my initial examination when I first woke up. Short cropped hair with a distinct kink, color indeterminate because it was covered with dust and soot. Scruffy jaw from not shaving for a few days, bulging biceps, the left arm of which was bound with a barbed wire tattoo that extended part way down his arm. Nice smattering of dark fur on his pecs with a trail that snaked over his belly and disappeared beneath his belt, making me want to explore further. Impressive package lay outlined in his jeans and I wished he'd turn around so I could get a glimpse of his ass. If it was as furry as his chest I would be in heaven if I could bury my face in his crack.

A chuckle made me look up. "Like what you see?" he smirked.

"Well, if you were naked I could give you a definitive answer." I couldn't believe I was letting my mouth run away with me. Before he could respond I shivered and sneezed loudly.

"Come on, mate," he said, "Can't have you catching pneumonia and dying on us."

Without waiting for an answer, he headed toward the tunnel.

"Hey, where are we going?"

"You'll see," he said as he jumped off the end of the platform and disappeared into the open craw of the tunnel. I chased after him but not before noticing how well his butt filled the ass of his jeans. "Wait up."

Shuddering with the thought that an early train might suddenly scream toward me, I jumped down and scrambled after him, losing my balance as stone ballast between the concrete sleepers bit into my bare feet. I tried hopping from sleeper to sleeper but they were hard to make out in the darkness, especially as my attention was more focused on watching out for an unexpected train that would spread my body parts for the next mile or two. I had no idea of the time, whether an early morning train was due at any moment or if it was still the middle of the night.

"Where are we going?" I shouted.

"To get you warm."

From the sound of his voice he was only a little way ahead so I ignored the sharp pain in my feet in an attempt to catch up. I had to assume he knew the railway timetable. I could just make out his body and fell in step behind him. "Bloody vandals," he cursed. "They knock out all the lights so the cops can't catch them when they scrawl their graffiti but it makes it fuckin' dangerous for us."

"So, what are you then? A sort of Phantom of the Opera…a Phantom of the Underground? You taking me to your lair?"

He stopped suddenly and I ran into his back. He turned to face me. "Why? Would you get off on that?"

I couldn't see his face clearly so I had no idea if his question was serious, amused, sinister, or any other permutation. I thought I'd go for the truth. "Yeah, I'd like that a lot."

I didn't see it coming until I felt his sandpaper jaw against my face. He was searching for my mouth and I immediately responded, pasting my lips to his. His tongue slid inside as he hugged me close enough that I felt his cock stiffen through his jeans. He must have felt mine do much the same. As his tongue explored every inch of my mouth, his arms inched their way down my back until he had his big hands clasping each of my butt cheeks. I heard him groan into my mouth as he squeezed. I took the opportunity, while he was distracted, to squeeze the thickness in his jeans. OMG! That would clear a few cobwebs.

When we finally broke in order to breathe, my voice quivered when I asked, "Who are you?"

He laughed. "Just an ordinary worker, mate. Maintenance crew. This line is shut down for the rest of the weekend so we can check and repair anything in this stretch of the tunnel."

I knew from bitter experience that every weekend part of the city's railway system was shut down and the trains replaced by a totally insufficient number of buses, seriously inconveniencing any plans I had for a party night out. I kept those thoughts to myself and asked the most obvious question. "You're not alone?"

"Nah, there's three of us. Roscoe and Marty and me."

"Oh." I must have packed a lot of disappointment in that one word because my man said quickly, "They'll like you almost as much as I do."

Almost?

"And you are?"

"I'm Hank. Foreman on this job."

"Hi, Hank. Pleased to meet you. Very pleased. I'm Landon."

"Well, Landon, it looks as if the gods have been kind to me, not sure if you think the same."

I patted his butt. "If it means I'm gonna get my tongue up that hairy ass crack of yours, then the gods are just as much on my side."

"Shit, mate, that image almost made me blow my load."

"That would be a pity," I purred. "I want to taste you."

He sounded surprised. "You swallow?"

"Every drop," I said proudly.

"Oh, man," he moaned. "He grabbed my hand to drag me along but felt me limp as my feet hit stone. "I'm such a fuckwit," he said. "I forgot you're in your bare feet. Here." So saying he hoisted me up in a fireman's grip and slung me face down over his shoulder. I didn't know whether to be offended or impressed. The choice was made easier when his hand began to pat my ass.

Okay, it wasn't the most comfortable way to travel but it saved my feet and I managed to tell him the story of my life – my sex life at least – in the time it took him to get me to his destination; a sort of makeshift camp with a fire burning in a large metal barrel, tools scattered at the side of the lines, the whole area illuminated with emergency lights that blinded me as we emerged from the dark. I could distinctly hear the throb of hammers against the ribbon of track in the distance.

Hank shucked me off his shoulder and sat me on a plastic stool, kneeling to examine the soles of my feet for damage. He lifted a foot to his mouth and kissed the sole. I don't know why but I thought it was the most romantic thing anyone had ever done for me. Then he stood, and without a word, unzipped the fly of his jeans and hauled out a cock so hard he could have hammered the rail tracks with it. Instead, he slapped it around my face a few times as I attempted vainly to get my lips around it.

"You like cock, boy?" he asked.

Like he needed to ask. "Fuck, yeah."

"Where you like it?" he asked standing over me slowly milking his prick toward my mouth as I watched the pre-cum smear over the head.

"Mouth. Ass. Anywhere."

"You a hog, boy? Sex pig?"

"Fuck, yeah." The testosterone in the air was threatening to make me monosyllabic.

"You like rough working man cock, eh?"

"Can't get enough."

For a moment the sexual tension was broken when he laughed. "You'll get more than your fill this time, mate. Trust me, you'll be begging us to stop."

"In your dreams," I sneered.

He'd obviously heard enough because he slammed his cock between my lips to shut me up as if I'd issued a challenge. He held my head in place and fucked my face hard. Sure, there was gagging and a bit of choking, but that was only until I got the gist of his rhythm and adapted. I opened my throat to welcome his prick as he shoved roughly inward and grabbed a breath through my nose when he pulled back.

"You're fuckin' good, boy. I can see you like it a bit rough. A lot of guys talk big but run for the hills when it gets a bit nasty but you're a real pig, aren't you?"

I managed to nod a little and mutter 'uh huh' before he cut off my breath once again.

My eyes watered, my throat was raw, my face was battered as he slammed his belly against my forehead, and my hair hurt from where he held it tight. I was pinned by his prick so I couldn't move – and I was in fuckin' love. My tongue did all the worshipping for me, sliding along the underside of his shaft as he bludgeoned my mouth, his moaning letting me know my efforts were succeeding.

"Take it, boy," he panted as he peaked. "Swallow all my hot juice. Drink it down, pig."

He stopped thrusting, holding the back of my head with both hands as he pushed as far into me as was humanly possible, his legs juddering as he emptied his balls down my throat. He held me tight until he regained his equilibrium before letting go. Air burst out of my lungs as I gasped for breath while I concentrated on his cock which still dripped liberal amounts of residual spunk. I leaned over to lick the head of his softening, but still substantial, cock. He shuddered as I lapped him up, attempting to force my tongue away but I'm a determined fucker when it comes to sampling the fruit of my labor. I wasn't about to let him go until I'd tasted every drop.

"You're really good," he muttered, gasping for breath. He sat with such force on one of the other plastic stools I thought it would shatter under his weight.

I beamed but added with a cheeky grin, "You've only sampled half the goods. I'm even better where it counts."

"Oh, man," he groaned.

"Where are these mates of yours?"

He looked at me with what I hoped was new respect. "Greedy fucker, aren't you?"

"Didn't you promise that I'd be begging you to stop?"

"Yeah, I guess I did. So, that wasn't enough and you want to try the others as well?"

"Jealous?"

I don't think that idea had crossed his mind until now. He thought about it briefly. "Maybe. But me and the guys share everything. They'll like you. That's okay. Long as you don't like them more than me."

What was with this guy? I'd just met him and already he was doing a passable imitation of cling wrap. Not that I minded but I'm just not satisfied with one man. Not any that I've found so far, at any rate.

I patted his cock before he tucked it away and zipped up. "Not likely, big guy."

Hank stood to extract a whistle from his pocket. He gave a few loud blasts before cupping his hands around his mouth and shouted "Smoko." The metal clanging from farther along the line and muffled sounds of someone woo hooing reverberated back through the tunnel. Hank poured water from a bottle into the jerry-rigged electric kettle that was as battered and bruised as his face. Eventually two guys ambled into view giving me enough time to examine them in detail before they reached the security of the fire.

They'd both opened the front of their safety vest because it was humid this far into the tunnel. They were both younger than Hank by about ten years although it was hard to gauge at this distance and in this light. "The shaved guy is Marty, the guy in the cap is Roscoe," Hank said when he saw my interest. "Marty is a mean motherfucker. Been married three times but they all left him. Can't keep a girlfriend more than a few weeks. Too tough on them. Doesn't beat 'em up or anything, just too rough in the bed department for most. Roscoe's a sweet guy, just getting into it. Pussy whipped by his missus who insists he does as much overtime as possible to support her bad habits. One of those bad habits is entertaining men while Roscoe's at work. I know because I was one of the fuckers she asked."

"Did you…?" I wasn't sure why I asked, it was none of my business.

"Nah. Pussy don't interest me."

I guess I couldn't stop my eyebrow from rising in surprise, and he saw it.

"Not every gay man is a panty-waisted fag," he said. "You of all people should know that."

I was genuine when I said, "I'm surprised you haven't been snapped up."

"Same goes for you."

"Who's that?" Roscoe called when they finally saw me.

"Just a stray I found on the station," Hank replied.

Marty looked me over and licked his lips. "New meat?" From his accent I picked him as a Kiwi. "Mighty juicy and fresh by the looks of him."

"Come on, guys, you'll scare him," Roscoe warned.

"This one don't scare easy," Hank said.

"You tried him out already, you bastard?" Marty didn't look pissed.

"Might have," Hank grinned.

Marty began discarding his clothes leaving them where they fell. "Woo hoo, I gotta get me some of that." He hopped as he pulled his work trousers inside out in order to get them over his boots. He strode toward me, naked except for his footwear and thick socks, his cock already bobbing rampantly from a mat of trimmed pubes. The rest of his body was hair free – he obviously shaved. I'm not normally into smooth men but Marty was an appealing exception. He was buff and beautiful, and didn't he know it. He tugged at his prick to smear the pre-cum over the head, playing with his nipples with his free hand. He was built like the proverbial brick shithouse, his upper arm tattooed by some sort of totemic Maori symbol.

Hank whispered, "Now's the time to run if you changed your mind."

No way was I running, I was drooling – from both my mouth and my cock. I wished I wasn't still wearing my jeans. Oh well, time enough to remove them later.

Without so much as a greeting, Marty made a beeline for me still seated on the stool. I attempted to rise but he pushed me back down by the shoulder and then rubbed his cock and balls in my face. "Lick it, baby," he commanded. "Lick it good."

I tongued his smooth balls, savoring the salty taste of his sweat, nudging his eager prick with my nose. I love the smell that comes from between the thighs of hard working men; it's an aphrodisiac. Stopping to kiss the head of his slime slick cock which twitched in expectation, I headed back to his balls, pushing his legs apart so I could get my head between so that I had access to his ass.

"Oh, you fuckin' little ripper," he exclaimed. "I think this bastard is gonna eat my ass."

To prove him correct, I began to splay his cheeks apart so I could bury my tongue between those tanned mounds of muscle. He leaned forward to give me access. His hairless puckered hole was beautiful and my tongue dove straight in, licking and probing until the tip wormed its way inside.

"Holy fuck, man. You got a magic tongue." Marty began grinding his ass into my face as if he wanted my tongue way up inside him. Amazing how many tops like that feeling. Maybe they're closeted bottoms, too afraid to try.

All I know is most tops don't reciprocate.

Marty was huffing as I dug farther into his guts with my tongue.

"Stop hogging the fag," Roscoe whined. "Give a bloke a go."

Hank laughed. "There's plenty to go round, boys. Don't fight over him: he's a stayer, not a bolter."

I couldn't speak as I had a mouthful of ass at that moment, so I gave the thumbs up to show I agreed.

"Still, by the time I have me dacks down, I want one of his holes. I'm horny as fuck," Roscoe warned. "I don't care which hole cause the missus don't do anal and she don't do oral, so I gotta get it where I can."

I was glad to be of service.

"Are we gonna throw him back where he came from when we get our rocks off?" Marty asked, "Or is he here for the duration?"

"He's here for the night boys, so you can sample the buffet as many times as you want," Hank said confidently.

"What if he don't wanna?" Marty asked.

"Too bad. See that rope over there? We attach him to one of the pipes that run through the tunnel until we've finished with him. If he don't like it, who gives a fuck?" Hank's words had me harder than I ever thought possible. "If he really makes a fuss, we'll leave him here for the guys on the day shift."

Holy fuck! Does it get any better than this? For a while I seriously thought about kicking and struggling just so I was roped to the tunnel, but then I remembered I like to have freedom of movement to stimulate my partners.

"That's it, mate. I can't take any more," Marty moaned as he withdrew his ass, allowing me to take full gulps of air. "I'd love to have you chewing on my ring all night but a guy's gotta earn a living." He turned and waved his drooling cock in my face. "Open up."

I swallowed his cock whole because I knew he wasn't far off blowing his load. Taking a chance I wrapped my hands around his ass cheeks, squirreling a finger toward his butt hole. I teased it with my middle finger, rubbing it and caressing it. He held my head and started to skull-fuck my throat. After an initial gag because he caught me by surprise, I managed to get my breath under control, opening up to take him. "Christ, this guy deep throats with no trouble at all."

I prodded my finger into his sphincter, parting it slowly. I felt him tense slightly but he must have enjoyed it because a few seconds later he relaxed to concentrate on getting his load out. I pushed a little harder and his ring, tight as it was, allowed me in. He backed up against my finger and with a little digital maneuvering I found his prostate, rubbing my finger over it.

That was enough to get him to scream a dozen obscenities that echoed off the walls of the tunnel. I felt his balls contract and then he flooded my throat with his cum. After the first three or four squirts I pulled back to get the remnants on my tongue so I could taste him.

"I can't believe he swallowed all my junk. Most chicks spit it out. That's when they even let you stick it their mouths at all. Can I keep him, Hank? Can I take him home?"

I knew Marty was joking but I'd be happy to end up in his bed any time.

He shucked his work trousers back on and whistling the latest pop hit wandered back along the rail with his mug of steaming instant coffee, promising he'd be back. "Looking forward to it," I shouted after him.

"I think it might be time to remove those constricting clothes of yours," Hank said hauling me to my feet so he could begin helping me out of my T-shirt. I unzipped and pulled my jeans down. I'd turned my back to both of them so they could see the asset they most wanted. My tight briefs hugged my ass. I bent over to pull my jeans off and I heard one of them whistle low.

Then I slowly peeled my briefs over my rump until they fell to my ankles. I toed them off before leaning forward and pulling my ass cheeks apart so they could see my snug entry.

"Sweet Jesus," Roscoe groaned as he fingered me. "So fuckin' tight. I don't think I'll be able to get this monster cock inside him."

That sure perked my interest and I turned my head to see what he was talking about. 'Sweet Jesus' was no exaggeration. There was a beer can with a head sprouting from his pubic hair. No wonder his wife didn't want it in her mouth or her ass. I think taking it in her pussy would have meant not being able to walk for a week.

"Don't scare the lad," Hank laughed. "He's probably never seen a deformity like you've got."

"No deformity, mate," Roscoe sneered. "It's all Grade-A cock."

"Think you can take it?" Hank asked.

"Is the Pope Catholic?" I replied with more bravado than common sense. I was pretty sure my sphincter could stretch to accommodate that fucker, but I wasn't certain.

Hank had the solution. "Let me go first. I'll open him up and then you can have a go."

"He can suck on it while I'm waiting," Roscoe said.

"Let's get him comfortable, at least," Hank suggested.

As they manhandled one of the wooden benches for me to straddle, I went over to my jeans to retrieve a small squeeze tube of lube from the pocket. No way was I taking these guys without some sort of help. I squeezed a generous helping onto my fingers and rubbed it around my sphincter before pushing inside. I lathered it in generously and when I finished I noticed the two guys were watching me with cheeky smiles on the faces. "This guy's a real professional," Hank smirked.

"I used to belong to the Boy Scouts and took their motto to heart. Be Prepared," I joked.

"You want it on your back or your stomach?" Hank asked, ever the practical foreman.

"I like to watch the guys fucking me, thanks for asking."

Hank lifted me onto the bench and hoisted my legs in the air. He had to find a small tool box to stand on so his cock lined up with my ass. While he was doing that, Roscoe pulled my head back and attempted to stuff his salami in my mouth. I was choking, unable to breathe.

"Take it easy, Roscoe," Hank said. "Let him do the work otherwise you'll dislocate his jaw."

I was grateful when Roscoe just held his prick near my lips so that I could lick around the head and slowly suck it between my lips. My mouth had never been stretched so far before and I hoped it was elastic enough to snap back into shape otherwise I would be left with a rictus grin.

Roscoe was obviously not used to expert cock sucking. I felt his body shudder each time I lapped my tongue along his shaft, slowly pushing my way along the length. My jaw ached but there was no way I would let this monster defeat me. Hank took advantage of my preoccupation by slowly easing his cock into my guts. He was a big guy all over although nowhere near as large as Roscoe in the cock department – but it stung nonetheless. He was in no hurry, allowing me to get used to the burning sensation before he slid all the way in to his balls.

Hank began slowly, enjoying the way I constricted my ass lips around his prick as he slid in and out, massaging my prostate as he did so. That left me to concentrate on Roscoe. My neck was sore from the awkward position and my head upside down was not ideal but I opened wide and took another couple of centimeters inside. I tried my best to keep my teeth out of the way but every now and then I felt them graze against Roscoe's shaft. He didn't seem to mind, in fact, it seemed to excite him even more.

I managed to push Roscoe aside gently. "In the pocket of my jeans. Poppers," I gasped.

He had no idea what I was talking about but Hank did. He pulled out which gave me the opportunity to stand and stretch my aching muscles. Much as I wanted to watch Hank's face as he plowed my ass, it was more comfortable on my stomach. I turned over as Hank came back with the small bottle. "Here, kid," he said. "You think that will do the trick?"

I smiled. "If I can't take Roscoe's cock with a bit of this sort of help, then I'll die trying."

"Don't want you dying," Hank said. "Not till we finish with you."

I offered him my ass and he slid in smoothly and then waited until I got myself ready for Roscoe. I took a couple of hits in each nostril, screwed the cap back on the bottle which I kept in my hand, and waited for the rush.

"Fuck my face now!" I screeched at Roscoe. He pushed his cock against my lips as my heart pounded and the blood carried the rush to my brain and my ass. With a superhuman effort I opened my mouth as wide as I could hoping to die choked on rock hard cock, and Roscoe slipped in farther than he'd managed before.

"No one has ever got it down to there," he admired.

I was determined to get it even farther.

Hank took it easy on my ass because he knew my concentration was on pleasing Roscoe's cock. I'd have to take a closer look at the man when all this was over. He was a good fuck, a hot man, and a considerate lover, not a combination I came across very often. Or who came across me, for that matter.

I slobbered over Roscoe's cock getting it slicked up so that it slid smoothly over my tongue. The rush wore off and I needed another hit for the final assault. I tapped Roscoe's thigh and he pulled out. I took two enormous snorts from the bottle of poppers, told Roscoe to 'go for it' and waited until he slammed his cock into my mouth. I'd taken a deep breath, I'd prepared my jaw as best I could and I felt the monster slip into the back of my throat. I wanted to puke from the effort but the rush kept me trying to suck every ounce of sperm from his balls.

Roscoe managed to wheeze, "Fuck, oh fuck, oh fuck. He's taken it all down his throat. Oh fuck. Oh, Jesus."

Hank picked up the pace, ramming into my hungry ass until I felt him grip my waist and slam me until I was totally kebabbed and unable to move. My ass overflowed with warm spunk as Hank unloaded inside me. Much as I wanted to get Roscoe off in my mouth, that would have just been showing off. Besides, I wanted that buggerator of a cock in my ass where it belonged. I tapped his thigh and he pulled out with a certain reluctance. "I want you in my ass, man," I said by way of consolation.

Hank pulled out, attempting to grease my ass with the cream that oozed out of me. Roscoe was an impatient bastard and as soon as Hank moved aside, he lined his cock up with my spunked entrance and pushed. I didn't just see stars; I saw the moon and all the planets as well as I screamed, "Fuckin' hell. I feel like someone's just shoved a traffic cone up my ass."

"Almost as big as," Roscoe laughed.

"Let me get used to it, mate, then you can fuck me any way you want," I suggested.

I squeezed my ass muscles around his prick and felt it twitch. I knew the burn would not last long. And it didn't. About thirty seconds after having that log lodged in my butt, it became just about the best feeling a pig bottom such as me could ever hope to have. I was in hog heaven. I took one last snort from the poppers bottle and then screamed to be fucked senseless. Roscoe was happy to oblige, obviously never having had a partner who could take him and beg for more.

Hank watched as he slowly milked his own cock. "Awesome, man."

My hole stretched to accommodate that thick hard weapon as it assaulted my butt. If my insides could bruise, this hot hard fuck would do it. Roscoe was a man of short thrusts, bursting his way into my bowels with his stubby thick prick. I attempted to push back against him, eager for even more inside me. My ass was on fire; my head swam from the best fucking I'd had all year. Roscoe pounded like a man starved of sex, grabbing my nipples and squeezing hard turning the pain into something so pleasurable I thought I'd blow my own load. I heard my ass squelch each time he rammed inside me, Hank's load slicking his entry. He wanted it to last as much as I did, I doubted even his wife took on this mammoth prick very often and Roscoe seemed to be making up for lost opportunities. I guessed he'd want another go that night. I wasn't sure my ass or my mouth was up to it.

Time to think of that later. Roscoe was headed down the home straight and I flexed my sphincter to give him as much grip as possible. He spat, he cursed, he bit into my shoulder blade in an effort to delay the inevitable but he bellowed his orgasm, squirting enough spunk inside me to grease a troop of bottoms. I slumped across the bench, totally worn out, feeling him fucking every last drop into me. It wasn't until he began to pull out that I realized I'd blown my load as well.

Roscoe slapped me on the ass, "Thanks, mate. I'll be back for more later." I didn't know if that was a threat or a promise.

"I'll be here," I muttered.

When we were alone, Hank helped me sit up on the bench. "That was some display," he said admiringly. "You are one cock hog. Think you can take more?"

"Of course," I boasted, thinking he meant later that night after I'd rested. More fool me.

Hank pushed me on my back, prodded his hard cock at my entrance and sank right in. I felt him, but there was no pain. He pulled me against his prick, embedding it as far inside me as it could go, and then began to bang me roughly – just the way I like it. He had a good mouth for slut talk, calling me every filthy name he could think of. I begged him to fuck my punk ass and the only thing that shut me up was when he pasted his mouth over mine and his tongue did to my face what his cock was doing to my ass.

I groaned louder than I ever have before. If I could have begged, I would have. I never got the opportunity until Hank shot a smaller load inside me. I didn't feel it that time but I knew from his gritted teeth and the grunts he was unloading inside me. He jerked my cock as he did so and soon my own cum splashed over my chest, my ass clenching around his cock. He slumped against me, our sweat and my slime sticking to our chests and stomachs. Hank held on like he didn't want to let go.

Eventually, he pulled out and spunk oozed out of me until my asshole sealed – admittedly a little less tightly than before. Hank handed me my clothes. "What's that for?" I asked. "You embarrassed to see me naked now that you've fucked me."

"Hell, no," he laughed. "I could look at you all day in the buff."

"Then why are you giving me my clothes?"

"I thought you'd want to get out of here before the guys come back. Especially Roscoe."

"Okay, I'm a bit sore but bring it on. It's been a long, long time since I had sex as good as you guys. One guy in particular seems to rock my boat a little more than the others."

I saw a sting of jealousy cloud his face for a split second. "Roscoe?"

I smiled because I knew I had read him correctly. "You, asshole."

His face lit up. "Yeah, well, I ain't never met anyone quite like you before. Cock hog. Slut."

"You can call me all the names you want. It just turns me on."

"You ever think about…you know…?"

I knew what he was asking but ignored the question. "You like watching Roscoe and Marty fuck me?"

"Roscoe's cock buried in your guts – fuckin' awesome."

"You're not the jealous type?'

"Only when a guy goes behind my back."

"Mmm," I purred. "Why would anyone need to with a hot daddy like you?"

He blushed. "Ah…how are you getting home later?"

"I was hoping you might lend me the fare. I lost my wallet somewhere last night."

"How about I drive you? Take you out to get some breakfast, then take you home."

"Like a date, you mean?"

He was coy. "If…if you like."

"I do like." So saying I grabbed him and pulled him against my sticky body pushing my tongue between his lips. He reciprocated just the way I like. He slid his fingers into my well-lubricated ass, getting me ready for his mates.

This was gonna be the beginning of a beautiful friendship.

BET YOUR STRAIGHT ASS

I was fucked. Not literally, of course. But, chances are, that fate was well on the way, although I couldn't believe my nemesis would follow through. If I had to fight for my virgin ass I knew I had some good dudes around me who would cover for me.

It was my own fault now that I look back on it. The confrontation had been brewing for some time. If it was going to happen, naturally, it would have to be that day.

I couldn't believe my luck. All fuckin' bad. Could the day get any worse? Oh, yeah. The mongrel bastard who was responsible for a lot of ill omens was seated directly across the table from me with the biggest shit eating grin in the universe. He had good reason. He had a pile of money in front of him, most of it mine. More than a month's wages, hard-earned from my shifts at the takeaway burger joint and stacking shelves midnight to dawn two nights a week at the local supermarket. I couldn't afford the poverty. Plus he also had smaller stacks of cash from the other guys in the frat house who'd turned out to play poker on that boring lazy Sunday evening.

Ivan was a cocky bastard, keen to see me fail. Delete that. Keen to see me grovel. He'd been that way since he gate crashed a frat party earlier that year and sort of never left. No one thought too much about it. He always had the best party favorites to share. The best chicks to share. The best everything to share. I couldn't compete. Didn't try.

I was head cocky at this particular frat house and I didn't need to buy my popularity. I was a stud of proven proportions having broken a few hearts, more than enough cunt virgins, and scored enough touchdowns for the college football team to be listed in gold lettering on their Scroll of Honor.

Now, there's always room enough for more than one alpha in the house but there can only ever be one alpha alpha, if you get my drift. Like, nothing's official. It just comes about through natural attrition, guys just silently acknowledge another dude's superiority, the way they all did me at Alpha Beta Pi. Meant things ran smoothly. No problems that couldn't be sorted out. I guess I was the Don Corleone of the frat house.

I only found out later that Ivan coveted my position and was white anting me at every opportunity. He wanted my crown. It's good to be the king. He didn't understand that top alpha is not a popularity contest, it's got nothing to do with democracy – it's all to do with power. I don't mean brute force 'cause Ivan beat me there. He was an enormous fucker. One of the reasons I'd been benched that day.

The most important match of the season and Coach Martin sent Ivan on in my place. Coach had balled me out earlier telling me my place on the team was in jeopardy unless I could get my shit together. "You're getting flabby," he said, scratching his balls like he had a groin full of crabs. He smacked my stomach for emphasis. That was rich coming from a guy whose idea of a balanced meal was doughnuts and ice cream, washed down with a non-diet soda. He stank of body odor and bad breath. The only thing that saved him in his job was his uncanny ability to produce winning teams year after year. Yeah, I guess my form had slumped but way to humiliate a guy.

My chick, Melissa, had been in the stands boasting to her BFFs about my prowess on a day I didn't get an opportunity to play. She wasn't waiting for me when I emerged from the showers later.

I guess Ivan took pity on me. He slapped me on the ass, squeezing my butt cheeks in a much too friendly fashion, before draping his muscular arm across my shoulders in a buddy buddy fashion I didn't feel.

"Come and join us for a brew. Wind down after that intense march."

Yeah, right. There's nothing more intense than sitting on the bench watching your whole life shredded, watching your teammates wallow in the glory that you'd help set up. Even more dire was watching the asshole who stole your thunder getting all the credit.

I went along with them even though I felt sidelined. The conversation was full of bragging and an in-depth debrief of the game to which I could add nothing, so I sat and drank, not pacing myself at all.

I'm such a clueless schmuck. I was three sheets to the wind by the time someone suggested we head back to the frat house for a poker game, pizza and pussy. Damn Melissa. If she wouldn't wait for me after the game then why should I save myself to tap her pussy? The testosterone was so thick after a winning game you could have sliced it and served it on a bun. Naturally, with a poker game you have to have a surfeit of brewskis – what else is a poker game for? Right? And there has to be a lot of sex braggadocio or what's the point of having good mates?

But the pizza order was for after the game and all that beer made me light-headed. Made me much too adventurous for my own good. So I was ripe for a fall when I bet on my sure-fire hand at cards. I couldn't be beaten. Not in my mood.

Ivan merely smiled at me across the table while Ken, Rick, Ray, and Marvin looked on glassy-eyed and seemed nervous. Little did I know it was for me at the time.

My best mate, Rick, grabbed my wrist before I could do anything more stupid than lose all the money I had in the world. I'd asked him for a loan.

"You've had enough, Andy. I doubt you can even see your own cards. Let it go. You've lost everything."

I could read the contempt in the other guys' expressions. Only Rick was on my side with perhaps a scrotum's worth of sympathy from my other buddy, Ken.

I shook Rick's hand off. "What sort of buddy are you if you won't help me out?"

"Maybe you've lost enough for tonight," Ivan commiserated. "Anyway, you've got nothing else to bet with." He began to straighten out his winnings into piles.

"Hey, there must be something I can wager against you. Help me out here."

Ivan shrugged. "You got nothing I want." He returned to arranging the cash. He took his time but I knew it was coming. He wanted to play this last hand as badly as I did. "Maybe…" He let it hang.

"Maybe?"

Ivan kept us all waiting. "You've got nothing of any value that I want, so maybe…"

"Spit it out."

His face broke out into the sort of grin you'd expect from a shark or a rattlesnake. "If you think you've got what it takes, then why not…bet your ass?"

There was stunned silence around the table. Rick tugged at my arm. "Come on, let's go."

"Wait a minute," I said, too blind to see the trap. I looked at my cards again. Fuck, I'd never felt more like a winner. "And…"

"If you win, this is all yours." He pushed the cash into the middle of the table. I could live on that for months. I guess that's when sense flew out the window.

"You've got a bet," I smirked, laying my cards on the table.

I have to hand it to Ivan. There was no gloat of triumph; he merely laid his cards out, waiting for my loss to register with my drunken brain.

"Holy fuck," Ken gasped.

"Clear that up for me, dudes," Ivan instructed Ray and Marvin, his followers. I'd once stupidly called them his 'fag boys' to his face and I don't think Ivan had ever forgiven me for that slight – even now. "Get Andy a beer," Ivan ordered. "He's gonna need it."

Ken handed me a cold beer and I swallowed half of it in panic. Surely…

Rick asked out loud what I was only thinking. "Surely you weren't serious about that bet?"

Ivan was calm. Too calm. "Would you have said the same thing if Andy here had won that round?"

"Well, no," Rick admitted.

"Why is it so different then because I won?"

"You know, man," Rick pleaded. "He bet his ass."

Ivan seemed pleased. "Yeah, how about that?"

"What can you do with his ass, dude?" Marvin asked.

Ivan snickered. "The possibilities are endless. I could bend it over my knee and spank it. But I think he'd probably like that. I could pimp him out to that fag frat to break him in, then I could fuck it." He adjusted his crotch which drew everyone's attention to the outline of a massive growth in his groin. The other four guys gasped. "Don't worry, I'll share him with you."

"I don't think—" Rick began.

"No, you don't," Ivan interrupted. "Otherwise you wouldn't be friends with this pussy. You want to welch on the bet, Andy?"

It was tempting but Alpha Beta Pi had strict rules about brothers not paying their debts to other brothers. It was almost certain banishment and total ostracism. I'd be out of the frat house and out of the football team. I'd be a pariah on campus. It was not an option.

I found my tongue at last. "You're not seriously going to force me to honor the bet?"

"There will be no force involved. You'll do it voluntarily. In fact, you'll beg for it by the time I've finished with you."

Rick sprang to my defense. "Come on, Ivan. This joke's gone on long enough. You've humiliated Andy, taught him a lesson, if that was your aim."

"You really think so?"

Ivan approached me, holding the neck of a three quarters full bottle of bourbon. He gulped a mouthful before offering it to me. "Here, it'll dull the pain." He held the bottle to my lips, prying them open with his thumb, pouring a tumbler full of alcohol down my throat. I felt something hard washed down with it. I looked at him in surprise. He winked. "Not so much I don't want you to feel it."

"Why are you doing this?" I spluttered as the liquid burned my throat and lit up my insides like the New Year's Eve fireworks.

"Wasn't it you that called me and my boys faggots?"

"You know it was a joke," I whined.

"Oh, what a shame you didn't tell me earlier," he said sarcastically. "Too late. Now we're gonna find out exactly who the real faggot is."

Ivan threw his mobile to Marvin. "Ring for the pizza. A couple of supremes, that should do it." Turning to Rick and Ken, he asked, "You staying for the…um…show?"

Ken was eager. "If there's pizza and beer, sure, why not?"

"And pussy," Marvin added. "Sweet pussy."

"We may not need it if Andy here has a pussy as sweet as I think it might be," Ivan said.

"Aw, faggot shit," Ray moaned.

Ivan clipped him hard across the back of the head. "You in or out?"

Ray grizzled, rubbing the back of his head. "In."

Rick made eye contact with me as if to suggest we make a run for it but I was so unsteady on my feet, my head spinning, I threatened to fall at any moment. I was hoping maybe he'd get help or ring the relevant authorities. Right at that moment, I didn't care because my body was incapable of doing anything.

"Show us your ass, Andy," Ivan commanded. It didn't sound as if he'd left any room for argument.

I wobbled to my feet, holding on to the table so as not to fall over. I attempted to undo the button that held up my shorts, my mind oblivious to where my behavior was leading, almost falling on my butt.

Ivan grabbed me and shucked me against the table, running his hand over my tight shorts-covered butt cheeks. "Careful, we don't want any injury to that hot ass." He laughed. "At least not before the fun starts."

Wait a minute; he just described my ass as hot. When did he ever see it?

It took a few moments to work out he would have had plenty of time to see it in the showers after a game.

All I wanted to do was lie down and sleep. I was manhandled and suddenly felt air around my cock and balls. This time as Ivan ran his hand over my butt, I felt his fingers against my cheeks.

"Smooth as a baby," he whispered. Leaning closer, he added, "You've got no idea how long I've wanted to tag your ass. If you hadn't been such an asshole we might have been the best of buddies, but you were always so uptight about being king of this shit heap."

He smacked me hard. I felt the blood rush to my butt cheek.

"Hop on," he hissed.

I needed help to clamber onto the heavy wooden table, realizing my ass was on open display as I lay on my stomach.

"Kneel up," Ivan commanded.

I struggled to get my knees under me so my ass was in the air. I couldn't keep myself steady on my hands so I just leaned my face against the wood, trying to catch a few minutes sleep.

It was impossible as I felt fingers prizing my butt cheeks apart and fingers prying at my hole. The digits prodded and pushed until I felt one squeeze between my sphincter muscles. It fuckin' hurt.

I heard Ivan chuckle. "He's an anal virgin. Makes it so much better for us," he announced to the room. "He'll need some sort of lubrication. Rick, see if there's any baby oil in the dispensary."

I knew my best mate would refuse such a request although it would mean a lot more pain for me. A few minutes later I felt a greasy liquid on my lower back, then it began running down my ass channel. Before it reached my balls, Ivan was stuffing the lubrication against my hole, slipping a finger inside me with much less resistance than before.

I gasped at the feeling of fullness in my ass. I was too intoxicated to feel my dignity had been breached. He kept inserting more fingers to open me up until it felt as if he was scrambling through my bowels searching for something he'd lost. I was about to ask what…

Fuuuuuuck! He must have found it because when he ran his finger across something inside my ass it almost sent me flying through the ceiling. My cock, already hard from the attention my butt was receiving, drooled from the slit. He ran his thumb across the excretion making me flinch from the painfully sensitive pleasure.

"That's it, faggot boy; squeeze those ass muscles around my fingers."

There was no use asking me to do anything, my body was acting of its own volition without any input from my brain.

I smelled pizza. When did that arrive? I wondered, too, what my frat brothers would think if they came into the room and saw me spread across the table with Ivan's fingers in my butthole. Still, it wasn't like I could do much about it.

Ivan pulled his fingers out and must have walked around to where my head was resting against the table top for I felt someone lift me up by the chin. I looked into his eyes and saw no pity there. I just wished I could shut down my mind to hide until this was all over. I gave no thought to the future, hoping that what went on in the room would stay in the room.

He rubbed his thumb along my lips. "Open up, fag boy. That's it, suck my thumb. Mmm, you like that." With a deft movement I could just see from the corner of my eye, he unfastened the button holding up his trousers and unzipped, pushing them to the floor and stepping out of them as he kept his thumb in my mouth. He obviously went commando because I saw no boxers or briefs, or even a jock strap.

"Kick that stand over here, Ray," Ivan said, and I heard the scrap of a wooden box as it skidded across the small room. Suddenly, Ivan was taller, his cock dangling right near my face. My mouth was empty and to my surprise, my tongue snaked out to lick the head of Ivan's limp prick which was resting on the table.

He patted me on the head, "Good fag boy."

I'd never tasted cock before, not even my own. It sent a frisson down my body. Here I was licking the cock of my most hated enemy while my best mates and his followers watched. I presumed they were there because Ivan's body blocked them from my view.

Ivan seemed content to wait; at least until his cock engorged to its full length and thickness. His prick was swollen and mean looking. I knew it would choke me if he pushed it in all the way. After licking the salty residue that was beginning to ooze from the slit, I closed my mouth in an act of defiance. I could see my obituary now if I were to open up as he demanded.

Benched jock chokes to death on team mate's cock.

What would my parents say? What would Melissa say? My reputation would be shredded. Hell, if I was honest with myself, it was shredded now.

Squeezing my nose between his thumb and middle finger, cutting off my oxygen supply, Ivan waited for me to open my mouth to breathe. I held off as long as I could but it was inevitable I would have to give in. There was nothing intrinsically awful about having his cock in my mouth. It didn't taste nasty, it didn't smell, it had a pleasing texture. I rubbed my tongue along the length.

"Don't even think about biting or you'll find yourself at the bottom of the lake with your balls missing." I sent my mind into sleep mode before another headline could appear in my brain. "Keep your teeth out of the way. And you're gonna swallow."

Shit. I hadn't thought that far ahead. It sobered me up quick smart. I attempted to shake my head in protest but Ivan held me still and began a slow fucking motion as he embedded his cock farther into my gob, hitting the back of my throat, cutting off my air supply momentarily. I thrashed about, as much as was possible while impaled on his thick weapon. I heard snickers from the other guys in the room.

"Don't panic, fag boy. Learn to breathe when I pull out, or breathe through your nose. I have no intention of killing you with cock even though the idea does have its appeal and you might consider it an attractive alternative to what I have planned."

I spat his cock out while he was boasting to his audience. "Get on with it, you bastard. I don't have all night."

"On the contrary, that's exactly how long I intend keeping you here, Andy. You'll be extremely sore and very sorry when it's all over, but I think you'll know who's boss."

As punishment, Ivan sank his cock all the way in my gabby mouth, choking me, making my eyes water and my throat puke. He held the back of my head until my pulse thudded in my forehead and I'm sure I started to turn purple. Just when I thought I'd pass out, he released me and withdrew, leaving me gasping for breath, my face awash with mucous and tears. He rubbed his cock over my face spreading the slime, carefully avoiding my eyes.

Once I'd caught my breathe again, he slid none-too-kindly back between my lips, increasing the speed of his thrusts until the catch in his breath warned me of what was to come. "Fuckin' beautiful mouth, fag boy. I can't believe you've never sucked cock before. My buddies are gonna love your throat. No chick has ever sucked me as good as you. If I didn't have dibs on your ass, I'd fuck your sweet face all night."

He was panting by the time he finished speaking. I closed my eyes as I felt the tension in his balls, preparing myself for the worst. No way did I want to choke on my own vomit and I knew – I just knew – the idea, if not the taste, of Ivan's spunk in my belly would make me throw up big time. His orgasm was a bit of an anti-climax when it finally arrived. Ivan huffed and puffed like a water buffalo on heat before he shot his load, most of it going straight down my throat so I didn't taste it. The residue that did land on my tongue wasn't half bad, the consistency of the glue we used when I was in kindergarten. Maybe I'd have to rethink my aversion to swallowing man spunk.

"Fuck, he swallowed it all," I heard Ray say in the background.

"Maybe you'd like to feed him some of yours, Ray," Ivan said.

"The deal was my ass and you," I complained.

"To do what I like with," Ivan gloated. "And I'm a very caring, a very sharing type of guy. I like my buddies to have the good things I have."

Ivan stepped aside and Ray stepped up to the plate, already naked and already hard as iron. His was a thinner and shorter cock so I hoped I'd be able to take him with more ease. There was no use objecting, Ivan would take no notice, so it was best to try to get this ordeal over as quickly as possible by co-operating.

"Let me just stretch for a moment, I've got cramp."

Hands helped me off the table and I stretched my arms and legs, then my back, in an attempt to unknot my muscles and get the blood circulating again. I was shocked to notice all the guys in the room were now naked, stroking their own cocks while keeping focused on my ass and my face, even Rick, who I trusted with my life although he looked shamefaced when our eyes met. I knew when it came right down to it, he wouldn't join in so I didn't mind if he beat off watching my humiliation. There'd be no going back if he stuck his dick in my mouth. I noticed his was almost as thick as Ivan's.

"On your back, fag," Ivan said slapping me on the butt to signal my break was over. I was grateful for the pause in our activity although I knew the worst was to come.

"Let's get this over with," I said with as much bravado as I could muster while I lay back on the cold table, my head hanging over one end, my ass over the other.

Ivan lifted my legs, placing them on his shoulders. I gazed up at him, appraising his power, his majesty, the strength in his arms and torso, his bulging muscles. Chicks must shudder when they see him aiming his mammoth cock at their swollen pussies. Just as I shuddered as he greased his cock, rubbing it up and down my butt canal until he thought he'd tormented me enough. He pressed against my asshole and began to push slowly.

At first, my sphincter refused to give, fighting to retain its virginity. It was a no brainer though. Once the full force of Ivan's body pushed against my poorly fortified hole, it was me that was going to give. The head poked through and he paused.

"Holy fuck," I screamed. "Take it out."

He didn't.

"Just relax. It won't hurt for long. Soon you'll be begging me to ram it harder."

"Dream on. No way will I ever beg to be your bitch."

"You seem pretty relaxed about what we've done so far. I don't hear you complaining."

"Would it do any good to complain, apart from giving you satisfaction?"

"No good at all."

"That's what I thought. So you might as well get on with it."

I must have pissed him off because the gentle prodding that he'd done previously to force his knob into my ass was replaced with a single thrust that buried him balls deep inside me.

I grunted, almost biting my tongue off in an attempt to contain the pain in my ass. It stung like the devil himself had shoved a poker up my butt. It burned like hell and there was no escaping it as Ivan held me firm, his cock wedged tight inside me, a grin of satisfaction across his lips.

I took deep breaths, thought about Melissa, anything rather than the log I had jammed inside me. My sphincter did the obvious thing and tried desperately to shit it out. But people are right, you do get used to it, although I doubted this was gonna become a way of life with me. When I relaxed, Ivan began to fuck like a piston, slow at first until he saw I could take it without grimacing and then picking up speed so he was making the table rock with his hard thrusts.

"You like my cock in your ass, don't you, Andy? I bet you've been a faggot all along, dreaming of the day you could have my cock in your nelly ass. Oh, dude, your ass is smooth as any cunt. Tighter than any chick I've ever fucked. You guys have gotta try him."

Ray, who had been hovering around the other side of the table, obviously didn't want to wait. He pulled my head back so that it hung upside down over the edge. I opened my mouth to complain and he took the opportunity to shut me up by sliding his cock all the way down my throat in one smooth motion. I'd been unprepared and choked. He withdrew until I coughed up enough phlegm that I spat on the floor by turning my head to the side.

"Take it slow, Ray. No need to injure the fag before we all take a turn. We want him to enjoy it as well."

"Do we?" Ray smiled.

Ivan laughed. "Nah. Who cares if he enjoys it or not?"

I felt some of the other guys crowd around the table and my hands were placed around two hard cocks. I knew it wouldn't be Rick I was jerking off. It had to be Ken and Marvin. I was relying on Rick to pick up the pieces that were left after my humiliating ordeal.

I concentrated on the good feelings in my ass, especially when Ivan angled his cock in such a way it brushed over something inside me that made me crave more. I was glad now that Ray had his cock in my mouth because it prevented me from crying out that I wanted Ivan's cock to pound me harder.

I did. I really did. His cock was making me see sparks each time it hit that button buried deep in my ass. Sex had never been this hot with Melissa. But then, she didn't have a cock, would never think to push her finger in my butt and wouldn't dream of swallowing my junk. Yeah, now that I thought about it, Melissa was pretty vanilla.

Ray dumped his load and I swallowed as much of it as I could but some still spilled out the side of my mouth, running down my cheeks. Ray pulled out but I was not going to be allowed any rest time. Another cock was waiting to spew its load into my belly. Marvin's cock was short and stumpy and almost dislocated my jaw in its hurry to feel my warm, wet mouth around it. I stretched my jaw as wide as I could but still had difficulty.

"Shit, mind the teeth," he complained.

"Don't worry about it, Marvin. The coach is on his way and he'll have something that will relax the fag."

"He'd better," Marvin grumbled, "Or I'll break this faggot's jaw."

Ivan grabbed my shoulders, pulling my head up to give me a break, ensuring I made eye contact as he pushed his cock as far up into my bowels as was humanly possible. My cock was hard and aching for relief. I put my hand around my prick to jerk myself off but Ivan swatted it away. "Not until I say so, boy," he commanded.

"Your pussy is so fuckin' hot. You're sitting on a gold mine. You could make good money with an ass like this."

I had no idea what he was talking about but anyone who strokes my ego gets my attention even when they won't let me stroke my own dick.

Against my better judgment, I was enjoying Ivan's cock in my ass and began to push back against him each time he entered me. He had a look of triumph the first time I did it. When I continued he said with that superior air that so irritates me, "I told you you'd be begging for it before the night was over."

"I don't hear no begging," I sneered.

"Oh, you will."

He picked up the pace, slamming me harder and harder until I thought we'd end up on the floor. With a roar that should have alerted anyone at home in the frat house, he spurted his load deep inside my guts. The flood of warmth inside me set me off and my cock pulsed five or six ribbons of spunk between us. Ivan remained stock still to catch his breath after he'd unloaded.

"That was fuckin' awesome," he admitted as he pulled his cock out of my ass, his cum dribbling out onto the table.

I sat up to catch my own breath and wait for my heart to stop beating fit to burst. I'd never had an orgasm like it. A knock at the door made me tense up because I knew it had to be Coach Martin.

Ivan let him into the room, locking the door behind him.

"Well, what do we have here?" Coach said in a less than friendly tone.

I was sweaty and covered in cum.

"You bring the makings?" Marvin asked.

Coach merely pointed to his bag. Marvin broke it open and set up the pipe. This was turning into some party.

Coach circled me, running his grubby fat fingers along my legs, squeezing my balls till I thought they'd pop like a ripe pimple. He pushed me back onto the table, parted my ass cheeks and before I could complain he had two fingers inside me, fucking my hole until I groaned.

"Virgin?" he queried.

"Looks that way," Ivan replied.

"Damn, that's hot."

Marvin was already inhaling the vapors from the glass pipe.

Crystal meth.

"I brought something special for pretty boy here on the table. A butt rocket. If he thinks he saw stars before this will send him into outer space."

Coach shoved the meth suppository up my ass. I watched while the others smoked. I had no great problems with party drugs although I'd never done meth before. I wondered what effect it would have lodged in my butt with all that man cream.

The tingle began about half an hour later. My ass was on fire with desire. I wriggled around the table while the men circled me, coach now naked with his long pendulous cock hanging down from under his paunch. My brain, which had up until then done a good job of telling me Coach Martin was gross, was now watching his cock engorge with blood hoping to get a taste of it.

I lay my head over the edge of the table wishing he'd take the hint. Slapping me with his large football sausage, I opened my mouth to suck in the huge head. It tasted nasty, but I didn't care. All I wanted was to feel it in my throat, taste its nastiness on my tongue. Before I swallowed it totally, I turned to Marvin. "Shove that thick cock of yours in my butt. I want to feel it, dude. Fuck my faggot ass."

He was already well under the influence and didn't hesitate to slam my hole wide open, knocking the wind out of me, the burn from his cock stretching my endurance, almost making me beg for mercy. Coach had tired of my mouthing off and dragged my head back so he could impale my lips. I wanted cock and I wanted it bad. Even Coach's smelly balls bobbing around my nose were exciting me in a way I never thought possible. His cock was the longest I'd ever taken and it more than tickled my tonsils as it wormed its way down my throat.

He was obviously in no hurry to dump his load which I knew was going to be watery and foul tasting. He teased my tongue by pulling out then ramming all the way back in before I could catch my breath, sadistically using my body in ways that disorientated me.

Marvin was hollering like a stuck pig as he reamed my ass. He didn't last long and I felt his cum spurt inside me joining Ivan's fermenting spooge. There was no one else to fuck me now except my two buddies. I thought Ken would have a go but not Rick, he was too loyal. I hoped Coach was virile enough that after he suffocated me with his cum that he'd ride my butt as well.

I felt a cock line up with my slimehole and push. Oh my God, it felt so good. It was thick, long and hard as fuck. Whoever was riding me liked it rough and brutal and my body was reacting favorably to the pounding. I sucked Coach as expertly as I could and I felt the sweat dripping from his body as he got closer to orgasm. I wanted desperately to see who was in my ass.

Coach whimpered as he shot his load down my throat. Fortunately, he was embedded so deeply I tasted little of his cum. It was as unpleasant as I thought it would be, but I didn't care.

I lifted my head once Coach had withdrawn to identify my favorite fucker. I was startled when I looked into the drug-crazed eyes of my best buddy. Rick was frothing at the mouth as he fucked me like I was a piece of meat and I loved him all the more for it. "Take my cock you filthy fag. I want you to know what it feels like to be fucked by a real man. You won't sit down for a week after I've finished with you. I want to shove my fist up your skanky asshole."

I lay back and sighed. This was so taboo. My best friend was shagging my ass, calling me the foulest names, describing the hideous ways he wanted to torture me. And I came in bucket loads. I'd never been so turned on in my life.

Ken did me with a little more finesse and Ivan took another turn. When they were all shagged out, my ass still had that itch for cock. My mouth was as desperate for spunk as an alcoholic is for his liquor. I was writhing in torment.

"Fuck me, he's insatiable," Coach said.

"Shove your cock in my hole," I begged, fulfilling at least one of Ivan's prophecies. "I gotta have cock."

"It's the meth," Ivan said. "But it gives me an idea. That gay frat house on the other side of campus. Coach?"

"Yeah."

"Didn't you tell me some of those fags offered to pay good money if you could set them up with one of the jocks in the football team?"

Coach smiled. "Yeah, they did."

"You think they'd cough up if we offer party boy here with his insatiable ass and let 'em loose on him."

"I think they'd pay a fuckin' fortune."

"What do you think, fag?" Ivan asked, all eyes turning to me. He had his thumb on his cell phone, ready to dial.

My answer was simple. "I need more cock."

ROAD HUMP

It was no use; the hammering in my head would not go away no matter how many aspirin I'd taken during the night to avert a hangover, or using three pillows over my aching noggin to protect it from the slightest vibration. I screamed "Shut the fuck up!" at nobody in particular hoping it might have some results, but it didn't. The hammering continued.

Peeling open one eyelid with my thumb and forefinger – there was no way I could manage to open it without assistance – I peered at my bedroom window. Was that sunshine? What day was it? Where was I? Where was…what the hell was his name?

The room was familiar, at least one-eyed it was. I looked again to make sure. Yes, it was my bedroom. By a process of elimination, if I brought trade home last night then it was either Saturday or Sunday. That meant I could sleep in until the hammering inside my head stopped. Please God, make it soon. I put my hand out tentatively to feel the other side of the bed in case there was someone entangled in the sheet. I relaxed; I was alone. I listened carefully in case the trick I'd brought home was in the bathroom. Nah, the house was too quiet apart from the infernal hammering. As I drew my hand back it grazed a rather starched section of the sheet. Oh, yes, at least there had been semen spilled, although I usually prefer it down my throat or in my ass not on the bed linen where it dries like, well, starch.

I felt my cock. It was sticky so I must have blown a load some time during the night. My ass felt good. I touched my butt gingerly. OMG! The guy had left his cock inside me. I panicked for a moment then realized how ridiculous my assumption was. I felt again. Nah, it was my large butt plug. There was a hazy recollection of sex toys involved in last night's adventures. I groaned. Now I remembered. I'd pursued Jack for weeks before I finally got him home only to discover he was a bottom. Well, damn it, so am I. Sure I can top like the best power bottom but not after so many beers and hard liquor and enough drugs to choke a horse.

Normally I would have thrown the fucker out on his ear but I was mellow from the E and horny from the ice or some other shit, and I wanted cock. Bad. I wanted it rough, rugged, brutal and if the guy was a little bit on the ugly side, so much the better. Fuck, I was still horny just remembering how catastrophic the evening had been.

Jack and I had sat and giggled upon discovering we shared a similar predilection for cock in our ass. His suggestion that we use my large collection of sex toys on each other seemed the most sensible solution under the circumstances, particularly as neither of us had wanted to venture out again to the bars on a blustery Friday evening. That's right, it had been Friday. So today was Saturday. I could still go out tonight and get laid properly. Such a pity about Jack; he had one of the biggest cocks I'd ever seen. At least he let me suck it but, according to him, it did nothing for him so it never got really hard. Not until I shoved my largest silicone dildo where the sun don't shine and he shouted for God to preserve him because it felt so good. God wasn't helping me any. Where the fuck are all the tops in this miserable city? Has everyone gone nelly?

Everyone knows what a good fuck I am, so why aren't they lining up at my door? Not only am I brilliant in bed, I'm also gorgeous. Trim little swimmer's body, not like those muscle-bound morons with testicles the size of peas from all the steroids. I've an average-sized cock that can do its duty when it has to or can flood an appreciative throat with its juice. A butt that is a perfect bubble and a dark cavern that's more inviting than anything a spelunker is ever likely to climb into. And, last but not least, I'm handsome as fuck if you want my unbiased opinion. I could have been a model. I wear my blond hair long so a lot of straight guys – especially when they've had a few – have mistaken me for a girl when I go to a breeder bar with the guys from work. Even a few guys from my place of employment have hit on me but I don't follow through; I don't shit in my own backyard. Pity, 'cause some of my work mates are hot.

I don't have any ink although I was tempted once to have a tramp stamp tattooed on my butt cheek, then I thought what it would be like when I was sixty. Not a good look. I do, however, have a bar through my left nipple. I think it looks sexy. In case you're too sensitive to ask, I'm twenty-three and I have a shit job in retail. Menswear in a giant department store; not even one of those city boutique shops with the loud music and the silent treatment until you flash a platinum credit card, plus a fitting room where you can disappear for a few minutes to give or receive a quick blow job. I know, because I've blown quite a few of those uppity sales assistants myself when I've gone in to try on a new pair of tight trousers or a shirt that shows my very ample pec tits. Let me tell you, those guys are not so uppity when they have their cock in my mouth and I'm siphoning all the juice out of their balls.

If that makes me sound like a slut then you'd be wrong. Hell, I want to be a slut but I just don't get laid enough. I can't even get an apprenticeship to train in Slut 101. My best mates Marcie and Scott are sluts. Yeah, Marcie is a real woman and, to make her sluttiness easier, she swings both ways. In fact she'd fuck just about anything if it gave her an orgasm. I know, for a fact, she once slept with a garden hose on the front lawn of her apartment block because she thought she'd found the world's longest dick or the world's skinniest python, I don't remember which. She really should give up some of the shit she takes.

Scott is her sometimes boyfriend and although he's slightly bi, he's well to the gay side of the equation. He fucks me on occasions when he's horny and I've done him a few times, but it's for relief rather than passion.

My point is that those two are out every night of the week whoring their bodies around and it's very rare they don't score. Me? I just troll the bars and discos on Friday and Saturday nights. Sometimes on a Sunday afternoon, too. I've been known to spend a delightful Sunday in one of the saunas worshipping on my knees, draining up to a baker's dozen of rampant cocks, or else lying on my stomach until my butthole overflows with ball juice. But those days are the exception rather than the rule. I guess you can see that I'm really just your early twenties horny gay twink. I know that sometime in the future I'll get sick of all this cock and balls and settle down, give up the drugs and alcohol, and move to the suburbs with a nice man and…die of fuckin' boredom. In your dreams.

There was no way I was gonna get any sleep with that racket in my head, so I got up, slipped on my mini-robe which scarcely covered my butt cheeks, my tackle drooping just below the hem, and went downstairs to make myself a coffee. Caffeine sometimes relieves my headaches. I made it strong and black, flopping on the lounge in exhaustion because of lack of sleep.

I was still wired from a combination of the previous evening's cocktail of recreational substances and booze, plus I was horny as fuck – that hunger you get when you'd hump anything that came within grasp of your needy ass – and the strong coffee wasn't helping one bit. In fact, it was making it worse. I squeezed my ass against the lounge, prodding the butt plug in farther, scraping it across my prostate, almost blowing my load. God, what a slut. I wish. If I were a slut, I'd have at least a dozen names on speed dial, or else I'd live in an apartment block like the nearby Vaseline Towers so all I had to do was knock on any door and offer my ass. Hell, if I were a real slut, I'd have a sling and a plastic sheet-covered playroom.

No, I'd settled into a yuppie enclave. An old working class area that had been taken over and prissied up by young professionals and the sort of queens who thought sex was only for the bedroom with the lights off. Not me at all. I'm the sort of guy who wants a spotlight, an audience, and a camera crew, with groans and dialogue that would make a porn star blush. Of course, there would also have to be a team of hot men to service my throbbing ass and a representative of the Guinness Book of Records to verify my super-slutdom.

Not gonna happen. The most men I'd ever had at one time was precisely two. And that hadn't worked out. They were more into each other than me so I doubt they even knew when I got out of bed to dress and catch a cab home so much were they in the throes of whatever it was they saw in each other. I was well on the way to being The Slut Who Never Was.

To distract my mind I switched on the TV but, being Saturday morning, it was cartoons or the latest pop music. It didn't help because suddenly I was itching for a romp with some of the boy bands or male rockers in the video clips, or wondering about the age of consent for fantasizing about semi-naked cartoon males in young adult anime.

It had to be a plot: everything was doing my head in. The hammering got louder and I was about to scream when it struck me that the sound was not inside my head at all but coming from the street outside. Good, that gave me somewhere to focus my frustration.

As I lived in an old Victorian worker's terrace that fronted immediately on to the street, if I peeked from behind my blind to discover what dickwad was making the racket that threatened to make my brain bleed, I'd be seen. It had happened before when I'd taken the local skateboarders to task for building a makeshift ramp right outside my door. They'd sprayed the front of the house with 'Fag' and other terms of endearment which I'd been obliged to pay to have painted over. A news and photographic report about the incident in the local inner city newspaper was vindication for me and meant the skateboarders now gave my house a wide berth, but it also meant I couldn't open my front window without the threat of verbal abuse being lobbed in by homophobic passers-by.

I rushed upstairs, priming my phone because the one number I did have on speed dial was that of the local council rangers. Okay, so there was a sigh of despair every time I rang, but at least I got results. I hated living like this.

I shifted the curtain aside in my bedroom to glance down into the street. Shit. It was a road construction gang digging up the footpath and part of the roadway. It was okay for them, they were all wearing industrial sound mufflers on their ears. What about a poor hung-over gay boy like me? Where was my protection?

My head was obviously not in a good space this morning. I'd had it up to my eyeballs with being disrespected by local louts, God, the weather, my drug supplier who was upping his prices every time I rang, and now road workers. It was time to act.

I was in a fury. Imagining myself as tough as Conan the Barbarian, I strode to the front door, flinging it open so that it crashed against the wall, rattling the glasses down the hall in the kitchen. There'd be a dent in the plaster I'd have to pay for but appearances were more important than my wallet.

I stood, hands on hips, glaring at the workers who, of course, had not heard my dramatic entrance because of their ear protection. In retrospect, it was probably for the best, because I looked more like Tinker Belle than Conan. Still, I had to make an impression. Putting fingers to my mouth, I gave such a shrill whistle that even the workers turned. The jack hammer stopped, mouths gaped open, and all attention was focused on me; precisely where I like it. I screamed "Shut the fuck up!" in my most Crawfordesque voice, and then stepped aggressively out onto the pavement to show I meant business.

Except there was no pavement any more. I tumbled ass over tit into the gaping trench where once there had been a footpath, lucky there were no jagged metal pipes or large rocks in the hole, merely clay and earth that broke my fall. I lay at the bottom groaning, wondering whether I'd broken anything. When I finally opened my eyes and looked up, I wondered momentarily if I'd died and gone to gay heaven, for peering down into the hole were four men of varying degrees of hotness, all of them nudging the high end of the scale. And those bodies... Yum!

It was only when they began to laugh that I realized that, no, I was still in the midst of Homophobe Central. I couldn't see anything remotely amusing until I realized I was still in my cut-down robe which had come loose, leaving my genitals on open view and that my ass sported a black silicone butt plug which, from the position in which I found myself, could be plainly seen. Attempting to cover myself modestly I merely succeeded in rearranging my discomfort by falling farther down the trench which, in turn, led to more merriment from my audience.

I heard one of them snicker, "What's that thing stuck in his ass?"

"One of those toys that fags use for anal stimulation," another replied.

"How come you know about such shit?"

"I can read, dumb ass, not just look at the pictures."

"Who you calling a dumb ass?"

"You, dumb ass."

It was like listening to kids argue.

"A little help here," I squeaked, attempting unsuccessfully to get up, flopping about like an insect on its back.

I heard a thump in the trench as a body landed near my head before I registered a large hand, attached to a hairy muscular arm, stretch out toward me. "Here, son, let me help you."

I grabbed the lifeline and shortly I was whisked to my feet effortlessly but stumbled against the massive body of muscle as I attempted to get my balance. An arm snaked around me to hold me steady, wedging me tightly between two of the most perfect pecs I had ever seen, the aroma of sweat and testosterone tingling in my nostrils. The guy was stripped to the waist; his overalls peeled down to reveal his rippling torso. I wanted nothing more than to run my tongue across every inch of his skin, ending up nuzzled in his warm, inviting pits. I looked up into a pair of bemused eyes that seemed to suggest they knew exactly what I was thinking. My ass twitched and I suddenly realized it was empty; I'd obviously expelled the plug during my humiliation. Now was not the time to go searching for it. I'd sneak out under cover of darkness and retrieve the bloody thing.

"You okay?" a deep masculine voice asked. It was a mixture of concern and amusement.

"Yeah, I think so. Just a tiny bruise to the ego."

"Ouch, that hurts more than a broken limb."

Not the response I expected from a road worker.

My savior called to the guys standing about watching. "Don't just stand there, give the lad a hand."

The youngest of the group proffered help, hauling me effortlessly to the rim of the trench. The other two men grinned mischievously, grabbing their crotches in a suggestive manner. On any other occasion I would have been begging them for it, but this was not one such occasion. I was battered and bruised and in need of a shower to clean the mud off. I must have looked a real mess. I couldn't tell whether the men's leers were genuine or yet another attempt to belittle me. I snorted my contempt at their amateur innuendo. "No thanks, I have standards."

The guy who'd jumped into the trench to rescue me, called sharply, "Okay, you blokes, give it a rest." With no effort at all he propelled himself out of the hole, on to the muddy edge next to me.

"Sorry, mate, we didn't know you were home. We knocked earlier but there was no answer."

That would explain some of the noises in my head. "No…um…busy night."

"Well, we wanted to warn you about the dig."

"I can see why," I said. "How am I supposed to get in and out of my house?"

"You got a back entrance?" my rescuer asked, totally oblivious.

"He sure does and from the looks of it, it gets used on a regular basis," one of the workers said to gales of laughter from the others.

"There's only this door," I replied, choosing my words carefully. "The back of the property joins the back of the house in the street behind."

"I'm the foreman," my rescuer said, ignoring the salacious comments and crotch squeezing behind him. "What we'll do is put some planks down so you can get in and out the front door while we work."

"Um, okay."

I looked to the front entrance wondering how I could jump across the gaping trench right this minute to escape the hostile atmosphere. The foreman must have seen my look for he swept me up into his arms, his powerful hand supporting my naked butt as my robe hung free, the other hand under my shoulder, to the guffaws of the men. He was so tall it was an easy stride across the trench to get me to my front door, carrying me across the threshold like a new bride. If it hadn't been for the whistles and catcalls behind us I could have snuggled into his body and remained there all day, happy to wallow in his strength.

Once inside, he kicked the door closed on the ribald humor, and then let me down, my body brushing past a thickening hardness in his groin. I didn't let on that I'd felt it, wondering what, if anything, it indicated about the boss's interests. I didn't dare chance falling to my knees to worship his body in case I'd got my signals crossed.

"Don't mind the guys," he said. "They're harmless. They don't mean anything by it."

"Thanks."

Thanks? That's all I could say?

He held out his hand. "I'm Jake, boss of that unruly mob out there."

"Ross," I said, wishing I could shake more than just his hand.

Jake was strikingly good looking. He had a well-trimmed goatee and moustache which made him even more masculine, if that were even possible, and a body that wouldn't have disgraced a professional competition. The little I'd felt of his cock as I'd slithered to my feet revealed that was competition material as well.

"Well, Ross. My apologies again. Sorry for the inconvenience. If you feel you need to put in a complaint about anything that happened, here's the card with the contact details. I wouldn't blame you if you did but I'd consider it a real favor if you overlooked the men's stupid behavior. It wasn't meant to be threatening."

I took the card but allayed his fears. "Thanks, but I won't need the card. Apart from a bit of embarrassment, well…" I shrugged.

"From what I saw, you have nothing to be embarrassed about." He must have realized what he said because he turned toward the door. "Um, as I said, we'll get planks laid if you need to go out–"

"Not until this evening."

"Okay. We'll be here for another week or so, depending on the weather. We're putting a speed hump in the road a few doors down but we have to relocate a few pipes before we can do it. Hope it doesn't disturb you too much."

My libido, never restrained at the best of times, was already disturbed by Jake's towering presence so it was a fatuous apology although he hadn't meant it that way.

He continued. "If the blokes get too rowdy just tell them to shut the fuck up."

I'd tried that and look where it got me. Alone in my living room with the hottest man I'd ever seen. Maybe I would try it again, but next time I'd look where I was going.

As soon as Jake left I knew I had to do something about the churning in my balls and the twitch in my ass. I scooted upstairs to the bedroom, positioning myself at the window, angled so that I could watch the men at work but so they couldn't see me. I'd already collected one of my dildos to replace the butt plug I'd lost somewhere in the trench, and had it bedded nicely in my anal canal, rubbing all those spots that made me see stars. I squeezed my ass on the high kitchen chair on which I was perched, forcing the silicone cock farther inside, the tip of it smeared with the residual nose candy that I'd just used to tweak my mood. By late this afternoon, I'd be screaming for cock.

For the moment, though, I'd just have to relieve myself, otherwise I'd be tempted to put a general invitation to all and sundry on the front door to enter and partake of my sexual delights.

The four men were quite visible on the street. It was a humid, overcast day and they'd all discarded their tank tops, which now hung limply from their back pockets. The older guy, around Jake's age – I'd say late thirties or early forties – was going to pot, probably from too many beers, but he was still impressive, his torso covered in fur, so unlike Jake's smooth hairless skin, his arms like slabs of muscle. The two younger workers were darker, Mediterranean DNA probably somewhere in their background, built like smaller brick shithouses but still enough to gain maximum attention if they walked into any gay bar dressed as they were now.

Okay, so they were homophobic yobbos who'd probably beat me up if they met me in a dark alley, but isn't it the ultimate irony that I'd use them as material to jerk off? Or was that just the ultimate in self-loathing? I didn't have time to consider that philosophical argument at the moment because my cock demanded attention. The workers were all fantasy fodder but my concentration was on Jake. He was so charismatic, I'd be having wet dreams about him for weeks. In fact, every time I saw the speed hump in the middle of the street, I'd probably get hard remembering the guy who'd put it there.

I'd lubed my fist to make it easier on my cock and soon enough there were loud squelching noises as I moved my hand up and down with increasing speed, wiggling my ass to push the dildo against my prostate, fantasizing Jake pummeling my butthole while I sucked the other guys and they blew their hot spunk all over…holy fucking shit! My orgasm was so intense I spewed my load all over my hand, the initial squirts rocketing across the short space to my bed, splashing down on the doona cover. That would be hell to wash out.

I moaned as quietly as I could and, as the last spurts oozed down my shaft, Jake looked up at my window as if he'd heard me. He smiled knowingly. Did the man have some sort of karmic connection to me? For the moment, I didn't care. I was washed out. I still had the buzz but I needed to clean up, get myself ready for the bars later.

The hot water in the shower prickled my body, cleansing the mud and the jizz off me until I felt so relaxed, but still horny, I knew only an army would satisfy me that night. I got hard at the thought but I left it, not wanting to waste any more nut juice on my fist. The shower was so inviting, I didn't step out until my skin began to prune and, even then, my escape was reluctant. It was still too humid to wear anything other than a skimpy pair of shorts I used around the house. They were not meant for company, unless I was trying to impress. They were threadbare and a size too small for me, but comfortable as an old boot, hugging my crotch and my ass as if the fabric was making love to my sexy salient points.

I flopped in front of the TV to channel surf mindlessly in the hope I could find something to keep my mind off sex, but the jack hammering outside and the incessant babble of voices in the background were a constant reminder that I needed a man, any man. Hell, I needed men. Tonight was the night I officially became a slut – or died trying. I guess it wouldn't hurt to jerk off again. That way I wouldn't come too quickly tonight and my ass could endure a lot more punishment. Sometimes, if I'm meta-horny, after the first ejaculation my libido dies a little and it takes time to get back in the mood. I was counting on the combination of party favorites and the fact I'd whacked out a few loads beforehand to be enough to grant me superhuman stamina.

My ass was buzzing from the candy my dildo had pushed inside, so that was taken care of, but my cock refused to play dead. I just had to rub out a new one. I chose a straight porn DVD, a gangbang the likes of which I wanted tonight. I didn't mind watching the occasional breeder porn, especially if the men were hot and plentiful as they usually were in the gangbang collections. The plot was simple, a woman is lost and stumbles – oh, so fortuitously – on to a building site and all the horny construction workers decide to help her out. Being a good sport, she wants to thank them in the most immediate way possible; she gives up all her holes which the men fill with gusto and disgustingly impressive amounts of semen. Don't you just love the sheer realism of porn?

Ensuring I had all the necessaries to hand, I unloaded into a tissue, wiping my prick before stuffing it back in my shorts. I must have been exhausted and fallen asleep because I was awoken by an ominous clap of thunder which sounded much too close for comfort. Lightning lit up the street outside, the rain bucketing down. The DVD was still playing on the flat screen so I had only been out for ten to fifteen minutes at most, albeit enough time for the weather to turn. I hoped the road workers had run for cover at the first sign of a storm because the street held scant shelter from a downpour like this. There were no shop awnings or bus shelters to huddle under. The few trees were unlikely to offer much protection either and not a good idea to stand under their pendulous branches during an electrical storm.

I wasn't surprised then when I heard hammering at the door. I opened it to a very disheveled and damp Jake who had to shout to be heard. "You got an umbrella or something the guys can use till this blows over? Danny doesn't like storms, you know, lightning and all that shit."

"Are you insane?" I yelled. Jake looked somewhat abashed by my attitude. "Tell them to get inside here. Now."

I saw the group huddled together like drowned rats under the nearest tree which offered absolutely no protection and made them a target for instant incineration if a power pole toppled or they had the misfortune to be the target of a lightning strike. Jake motioned to them and the three grateful workers ran for the door dripping all over the tiled entrance.

"You got an umbrella?" Jake asked.

"There was one in the hall stand. Aren't you staying?"

"The truck is open to the rain. Got to close it up before anything gets damaged."

I handed him the umbrella, telling him I'd leave the door unlocked so he could let himself back in, and he disappeared out into the wet. I turned my attention to the three remaining drowned rats.

"Guys," I shouted over the general hubbub of thanks, "If you wouldn't mind remaining here, you can drip all you like on the tiles. I'll get you some towels and if you strip off those wet clothes I can pop them in the dryer so they'll be nice and dry by the time the storm blows over."

"You just want to see our cocks," the oldest retorted.

I wasn't gonna let these guys shit on my hospitality. "Listen, dickwad, I've seen enough cocks in my time, what makes you think your little pot-bellied effort will impress me? But, suit yourself. You can stand here with your dignity intact and your clothes wet through, or you come inside, after you've shed your clothes and I've given you a nice towel to dry yourself and wrap around your insecurity. Your choice."

One of the young guys began stripping. "Dickwad there is Brad, I'm Tony, and this is Danny. And if you truly believe you've seen everything in cock size there is to see, I doubt you've ever seen anything like Jake's."

Really? My mind went into overdrive imagining such a thing, but I was distracted by Danny who was shivering, whether because he was damp or frightened by the storm, I wasn't sure. "I'll be back in a moment." I belted upstairs to grab all my available towels and then ran back downstairs. Tony was already stripped, his cock hanging invitingly over an egg-sized set of balls. He saw me looking. "You like what you see?" He lifted his semi-tumescent shaft up in welcome.

"Impressive," I purred.

Tony was helping Danny out of his wet things while Dickwad was still obviously contemplating his options. I gathered up the soaking mess and carried the first lot to the laundry where I got the excess water out by bundling them into the washing machine and regulating it to spin dry. By the time I got back to the entrance hall, Danny had the towel wrapped around his waist, and Dickwad was reluctantly peeling off his clothes as he sneezed. Deciding to give them a little privacy, I asked, "Beer or coffee?"

It was unanimous. "Make yourselves at home in the living room while I get you all a beer." I disappeared into the kitchen raiding the fridge for their drinks and adding some crisps and other savory snacks in case they were hungry. I was reminded that I'd neglected to turn off the DVD player when I heard a shout of 'woo hoo' from Tony. "That's what I call making a person feel welcome." I wasn't sure whether he was referring to the fact I'd forgotten to turn off the porn, or whether he meant the manner in which the construction workers were making the woman feel welcome.

I took the drinks and snacks in on a tray and went to get the remote control. "Leave it on, man. This is what I call great entertainment," Tony said. I glanced at his towel, noticing it was having difficulty hiding his excitement. Danny and Brad were staring at the screen boggle-eyed and equally excited. I didn't for a moment think it was going to lead to anything so I discreetly excused myself to attend to the drying. Before I left the room, Tony asked sheepishly, "You mind if I...um..."

I had a fair idea what he was asking.

"Whack one out?" I asked.

"Yeah."

I pointed. "There are tissues. Try not to get it on the carpet. Aim for the coffee table."

"So you can lick it up later?" Tony winked. I blushed. Was I that transparent? "Thanks, man."

I fled. The first load had gone through the spin cycle so I moved it to the dryer and deposited the second load of wet in the washing machine. I waited for the second lot to spin dry, adding it to the dryer, allowing the guys enough space to feel comfortable. They probably thought I'd put the porn on to seduce them even though I'd had no such opportunity when they knocked.

I went back to the living room. The DVD was nearing the climax in more ways than one. Tony had peeled off his towel and was squeezing his balls, moaning 'oh, man' over and over like a prayer, as he milked his substantial cock. Danny and Brad had their hands under their towels to cover their modesty. I couldn't take my eyes off Tony's glistening cock. It was a thing of beauty and I wished I was down on my knees slurping it all into my throat.

With a shout of 'Goddam,' Tony blew a copious load all over his abs and his fist, startling his two companions. "Fuck, that was good," he panted. He looked around, smiling when he saw my eyes riveted on his prick.

"I'll get you a...um...warm wash cloth to...ah ...wipe that up," I stuttered.

"Nah," he said. "Why don't you just come over here and lick it off."

Brad and Danny stopped jerking when the movie clicked off; they now turned their attention to the interplay between their workmate and me.

I hesitated.

Tony wasn't about to take indecision for an answer. "Did you hear what I said, fag? Down on your knees, lick every bit of my spunk off my belly and my hands."

I didn't hesitate this time. If there was trouble later, Jake could bail me out. I kneeled and Tony pointed his cock at my mouth. I put my lips to the slit suctioning out the last oozing remnants of his ball batter, then tongued my way down to his sticky fist. He let go of his shaft so I could take each finger in my mouth, sucking it clean as if it were a thin dick. From the corner of my eye I noticed Brad and Danny watching closely.

Tony wiped the back of his hand over my face, rubbing the warm spunk into my skin. When I'd finished cleaning up his cock and his fingers, he pressed my face to the cum puddled in his abs. I lapped at it like a cat laps milk; swallowing his sweet, salty nectar as if it were the food of the gods. "Good boy," Tony said. "Now let me see you take care of my mates here." He leaned over and peeled the towel off Danny's crotch. His cock sprang free and hard. I wasn't sure Danny was up for a blow job but that decision was taken out of my hands when Tony kicked me along on my knees and forced my face down on the leaking cock.

I felt no fists rain down on me in homophobic panic, but I did feel Danny buck as my lips slid over his knob, so I relaxed into the task ahead. I hadn't had the opportunity to demonstrate my expertise on Tony because he'd already shot his bolt. Danny was a different matter altogether and I was determined to give him a good time. He attempted to force his cock farther into my mouth. I took a deep breath and allowed his prick into my throat. "Fuck," Danny gasped. "He can deep throat."

"I told you he'd be a total slut," Tony crowed. "I bet there's nothing this fag won't do to get cock."

I couldn't tell him he was spot on because at that moment my mouth was full. Using my tongue, my lips, the suction in my cheeks, every trick of the trade that I knew, it wasn't long before I felt that tell-tale clutch in the balls, and Danny began to whimper a warning. I had no intention of spitting so I pushed my mouth as far down on his cock as I could go, feeling it penetrate well into my throat, keeping my gag reflex at bay until I felt the machine gun squirts of cum. I pulled back to get the last few spasms of spunk on my tongue in order to taste him. Danny lay back against the lounge, totally depleted.

"Your turn, Brad," Tony said.

I thought there might be trouble but Brad already had his cock out, caressing it slowly as he watched me work on his mate. I sidled along until I was between his meaty thighs, my nose buried under his balls. I licked up and over his sac, nibbling up his shaft until I had him squirming. Once I'd run my tongue around the head of his prick, I had him. The tension I'd felt in his body dissipated and I went to work on his thick, stubby cock. It stretched my lips, and it took all my concentration to keep my teeth retracted, so I didn't know what Tony was up to until I felt something wet and cold against my butthole.

I looked briefly behind me to see Tony with the lube I keep in the kitchen to save me going upstairs if I bring trade home for a quickie. He massaged it into my anus. Raising my ass, I gave him better access to show I was more than willing because he was still sporting wood even though he'd blown a load less than ten minutes earlier. Brad held my head down as he slam fucked my face which meant I didn't notice Tony's cock until he rammed it to the hilt into my barely prepped asshole.

I saw stars but I had no time to adjust to my position as Tony held my waist and slammed into me repeatedly. "You got a tight ass, fag. I could fuck it all day. Breed you like a slut whore." He had a nice line in porn dialogue, which I enjoy, while Brad did everything in his power to keep even the minutest sounds of his enjoyment to himself; but I heard them. He obviously wanted to keep up his bullshit pretense.

I didn't care; I was in cock heaven. By this time I had weathered the worst of Tony's anal onslaught and pressed back against him each time he rammed past my sphincter to penetrate to his balls. It was not a method I usually liked but he was an expert at it, stretching my entrance until I thought it would snap. I picked up my pace and slammed my face down around the complete thickness of Brad's prick, daring him not to come, matching the rhythm of Tony's battering ram in my guts.

It worked and, as I felt Tony's load squelch into my ass, Brad finally wailed that he was coming, flooding my mouth and throat with his viscous sperm. I swallowed gratefully, like a starving man as I squeezed my ass muscles around Tony's pulsating prick.

"Is this a private party or can anyone join in?"

I looked up. Jake had obviously come back and stripped off in the hall for he was stroking his cock as he watched the action from the doorway. "Much better than a porno," he said.

I couldn't help but be impressed by the prodigious weapon he was holding. It was only a slight exaggeration to say he looked almost as if he had a third leg. I don't mean it was grotesque but it was the largest cock I'd ever seen outside a porn movie. It was between nine and ten inches, and thick. Not that ridiculous thick-as-a-Coke-can you read about but never stumble across, but certainly thicker than Brad, and I thought, to my horror, thicker than would ever fit in my ass let alone my mouth.

"I'm just loosening him up for you, boss," Tony said, withdrawing his prick, wiping the residue on my butt cheeks.

"No way can I take that monster," I complained. "It'll kill me."

"No one's died yet," Jake said with a twinkle in his eye. "Not that I can get the whole thing into many people. You know how frustrating it is just to get the head in and fuck them with that?"

"Very frustrating?" I offered.

"And very unsatisfying." He turned to his workers. "The rain's stopped, guys. You can take off if you want. Tomorrow's Sunday so I'll see you back on the job first thing Monday. Ross here might even invite us in for a morning…um…coffee, if you ask nicely."

"Any time you're in the neighborhood," I suggested. "If you're looking for your clothes, they're in the dryer in the laundry."

Brad and Danny both scampered. Having blown their loads, they were probably now fighting an attack of the guilts. Tony, on the other hand, didn't seem to have a guilty bone in his body.

"You staying?" Jake asked.

"Help you set it up, and then I might shoot off. I got a heavy date with Bronwyn tonight."

"Give her my best, will you."

"She keeps asking when you're coming over for dinner again."

"So she can set me up with that friend of hers. No thanks, I don't do pussy."

"I keep telling her, but…" Tony shrugged.

"I think we should let Ross control the pace," Jake said as if I wasn't in the room.

I still wasn't convinced that thing would fit in my tiny little hole without snapping me wide open.

Jake lay on the lounge, his cock poking up proudly like a gristle version of the Eiffel Tower. I lapped at his balls, slicking them with my spit before launching into the daunting task of running my tongue along the heaving shaft until I reached the summit. Sucking the slit which was already erupting precum, I tasted Jake for the first time. I could easily become addicted to his spunk. With difficulty, I managed to wrap my lips around the head of his prick, dreading to think what damage it would do to someone who was not as well-trained as I was.

I took my time, accepting a little more and a little more each time I bobbed my head, giving my jaw a rest when it became too painful to continue.

"This guy is a real slut," Tony said as he watched. "I don't think I've ever seen anyone so determined."

"Feels good, too," Jake purred watching me at work between his legs as he lay his head on his muscular arms.

I moved up to his pits, sniffing them until I got Jake's scent in my nostrils like I was a tracker dog. I licked the sparse hairs, sucking his salty sweat down into my belly. He growled in satisfaction. I attacked the second pit, repeating the ritual as I ran my hands appreciatively over his pecs which I tweaked with my finger nails until he writhed under my touch, then down over his six-pack until I snared his prick in my fist giving it a few tugs to let it know it hadn't been forgotten.

"You know, guys," I said, wondering whether what I was about to say would bring the whole sexual house of cards tumbling, or take it to a higher level. "I have a few recreational substances which will make this so much easier for me which will mean more pleasure for you."

"Bring it on," Tony said enthusiastically. "You okay with that, Jake?"

He shrugged. "If it helps."

I retrieved my stash and Jake and Tony iced my ass. It didn't take long for the buzz. Tony was a connoisseur, while Jake was a little more tentative. We had another round of beers before my ass twitched, telling me it was more than ready, no longer fearful of that monster erection that simply refused to go down.

I had something to prove, if not to Jake, then to myself. I kneeled between his legs, my ass raised to give Tony a chance to lube it with the cold gel. I got half of Jake's cock on my mouth but the remainder was proving difficult. My eyes were watering, my throat was raw, and strings of drool were hanging from my lips. "That is so hot," Tony panted as he watched. He had three fingers in my ass, screwing them in and out in an attempt to open me up. The ice buzz took me into another dimension and I wanted to be impaled on cock. I didn't care whether it choked me or split me open, I wanted it inside me. I got two thirds of Jake's cock into my mouth and throat and kept it there longer than I thought I could.

"Holy fuckin' Christ. You've swallowed more of me than anyone else ever has."

Gasping for breath, I managed to say, "Stay tuned. I'll suck you down to the balls eventually."

Tony had four fingers in my ass and it felt like I was being impaled on a fire hydrant but still I backed up for more. I felt insatiable. "I think he's primed and ready."

Jake held his cock aloft, slathering it with lube, as Tony helped me squat over it, holding me steady as I lowered myself. I felt Jake's glans brush my widened hole. "Just as well you use a butt plug, boy; otherwise you'd never be able to take me."

"Shut the fuck up and get on with it," I said, a little too cocksure of myself. It was uncomfortable squatting in this position for too long. If I stumbled I would impale myself on his prick and probably not settle until my ass hit his balls, my sphincter muscles snapping like an old rubber band.

I took a deep breath and pushed down until I felt the head of Jake's prick push aside any resistance and the head popped inside me. Nothing prepared me for the initial burst of searing pain. That must be what fisting is like. And Jake wasn't anywhere near as thick as your average hand. I paused until my libido took over and Jake's cock was all I wanted. I wanted it inside me. Now.

"That's it, fag boy," Jake encouraged as I bobbed slowly up and down, lowering my ass slightly with each stroke, clasping my muscles around his hardness. "You're so fucking tight," he moaned. "If you don't stop what you're doing you'll make me come."

I was sweating profusely from the exertion. "Isn't that the idea?"

"Not so soon. I want to enjoy this. Not many people out there can take me for more than thirty seconds to a minute."

"You're mixing with the wrong crowd. There are lots of sluts out there who could take you for hours on end."

"Yeah, but none of them are as cute and built and slutty as you are."

"Did you just call me cute?

"Uh huh."

"And built?"

"Uh huh."

Each time he nodded, I forced my ass pussy farther down his shaft.

"And slutty?"

"Uh huh."

I slammed my butt down until I thought I would burst. "Jesus fucking Christ," I screamed. I felt his pubes brush my ass cheeks. He was all the way in.

"I don't believe it," Tony said admiringly. "He's taken it all. What a slut."

"Thanks. That's been my life's ambition. To be a slut."

"I admire ambition in a young man," Jake grunted.

When the throbbing in my ass subsided, I lifted myself up gingerly before the long slide back down. Within a few minutes, I was in a frenzy to stuff more of Jake's cock in my butt. I bounced on his prick as if trying to snap it off at the balls and keep it inside me like a giant dildo. "How about we change positions now that I've got used to it?" I suggested.

"What position?" Jake asked.

"Me on my back, you between my legs so I can watch you as you spear me."

I lay down and Jake lifted my legs in the air.

"Wow, look at that gape," Tony said as he fingered some more lube in my battered hole.

Then Jake placed my legs on his shoulders and began to sink his cock into my greasy hole. He slipped in easier this time, his balls slapping against my ass in record time. He pulled back until just the head of his prick was inside my bowels and then sank all the way back in again. It was a smooth action which did unmentionable things to my prostate.

Tony must have forgotten his promise to keep something in reserve for his girlfriend because he was jerking his cock like a madman as he watched. "Un-fucking-believable. He took it all."

Not only could I take it all but the buzz kept repeating in my brain that I wanted to take it all night, until I was fucked senseless.

Jake increased his pace but not enough to satisfy me. He seemed almost afraid that he'd split me in two, I smacked his ass. "Come on, fuck me harder. There's no speed hump in my ass."

He took that as his cue to really ram me into the lounge, punishing my doubled over body until I thought my legs might snap off. Still, I cajoled him on to further feats of rough sex until I felt battered and bruised, my asshole begging for a break. My sphincter gripped him as he thrust in and thrust out until I heard the extra breaths he was taking and I felt his hot spunk flood my guts.

"Take it, you filthy fuckin' fag slut," he spat. "You're my slut now. You'll take my cock and my cum whenever and wherever I want. Understand, slut?"

"Yes, sir," I whimpered. Cum shot out of my prick as I brought myself off.

Tony added a few more expletives and a lot of foul talk as he spewed his balls out all over my face, rubbing the final drools across my lips.

Jake rammed a few last vestiges of spunk into my ass then fell against me until I thought I was going to be crushed or else my legs would go to sleep. He surprised me when he pushed his lips against mine, ignoring Tony's spunk, to plant his tongue inside my mouth. He was planting his flag, as well as his seed, proprietorially.

"Thanks, guys. See you Monday, Jake," Tony said as he headed to the laundry to get his dry clothes.

Jake withdrew, holding a towel under my ass to catch any overflow as his cock popped free. "That was intense," he said.

"Tell me about it."

"You want to go out or order in?"

"Order in. I don't think I can walk yet."

Jake sort of assumed control at that point. Over pizza and beer, he let it be known that I was now his slut. That was okay for the night because I was still high, but I wasn't so sure about the following day.

"I like sluts," he said. "I can't do the monogamy thing."

"Neither can I," I agreed.

"But I need to be in charge. I don't mind watching other guys fuck you from asshole to breakfast," he explained, "But only when I say so. Did you mean what you said about your ambition?"

"To be a slut, you mean?"

"Yeah, that."

"Yep, I did."

"Good, because I know a porn cinema where I'll take you and you'll put out for everyone who wants to fuck you or who wants you to suck their cock. And I know a building site where they'll shackle you to the fence and use you in ways you can't even imagine yet. You in?"

I didn't have to speak; I merely stood up and showed him how hard my cock was at the thought.

"This is a marriage made in heaven," he laughed. "You'll be a true slut in no time at all with my training."

"So this is a sort of apprenticeship?"

"You could call it that."

Yes!

For those who like to keep tabs: although we searched thoroughly we never did find my missing black butt plug, and it was the next day, Sunday, around 6PM when I finally managed to take his cock all the way down my throat to his balls.

BUTT ROGERS
IN THE 21ST CENTURY

It's funny how life can change on a whim. I suppose that's a cliché, but if I hadn't been working that night I wouldn't be the person I am today. I like the new genetically modified me, although I'm not sure I'd be up for eating a genetically modified burger if it was made from some of my body parts. But nobody's likely to eat me so I thank modern science that I have a life, because it wasn't always that way.

It began the day I was born, like all good stories do, though I'll skip the details of the first twenty-seven years and get to the point, the part that you're interested in. I need to sketch in a little about me first, though.

I suppose many people would see me as a loser. I prefer to call myself a dreamer. I'm not your typical nine-to-fiver, that would bore me rigid, whereas if I'm bored rigid I prefer it to be up my ass. My asshole is the center of my known universe. I'm always looking after its needs and not always as fussy as I should be about what I feed it. Cock, tongue and cum is its usual diet, occasionally silicone in the form of a dildo or else plastic in the form of a vibrator, much less often a fist or part of a foot.

So sue me, I'm adventurous.

If I don't have your usual stultifying job, what do I do? I can proudly boast I work in an adult book store, a sex shop, four nights a week. I work the night shift from 11pm to 7am, Thursday through Sunday. It doesn't pay all that well, just enough for my bedsit rent, my food and utilities with enough left over for cultural pursuits to feed the mind. Graphic novels. Comics, if you like. Particularly those about superheroes.

I sit behind the counter of *Anything Goes*, the city's premier adult bookstore, where most of my late-night customers are sex workers of all persuasions who hire our back rooms by the hour to avoid doing their business in the streets, or late partying gay boys who want to top up their supply of poppers. Anything they require in the way of harder drugs, I direct them across the street to the porn cinema where the ticket seller does a nice side trade in recreational substances for which you need a prescription. Or else a term in jail.

Don't get me started on that shit. I can't afford a criminal record.

The job offers me every opportunity to indulge my predilection for cock as well as supplying me with an endless procession of porno DVDs and magazines of all persuasions. You also get to meet the most interesting people, as well as the most delicious cocks and asses. Especially after the bars close and the gay boys who haven't found a partner make their way to the store to relieve themselves through the 'ventilation' holes carved in the porno booth walls or via their own hands.

I like to think of myself as a social worker and many's the time I've been down on my knees, my mouth glued to the glory hole as some anonymous punter squirts his load down my gullet, or else I back my hungry ass against the knob protruding from the adjacent cubicle. I don't do sex, I do quickies.

You may think that there's not much satisfaction in that but I'm here to tell you quantity beats quality every time. Not that I haven't done quality as well but quality takes time and patience, something I have in short supply. Time takes me away from valuable moments that could otherwise be spent reading comic books.

Some of the club boys can be mighty finicky about who they stick their cock into, although most really don't give a shit in the early hours of the morning. They just want a hole that's wet and warm so they can relieve their sexual stress and get a good night's sleep.

My favorites, though, are the married men who descend on the shop early Sunday morning. They leave their apartments dotted around this part of the inner city to wander down to the early opening patisseries to buy croissants and coffee, as well as the Sunday papers, to take back to loving wives, sometimes husbands. They usually have enough time to pop in to get taken care of by yours truly. I drain their balls and they go home happy. Probably saved many a squalid argument at the breakfast nook. The regulars are a friendly bunch and will happily wait around chatting if there's a traffic jam for my throat or ass, preferring that to the more solitary delights of masturbation.

My official title is Night Manager. I even have a badge pinned to my scruffy T-shirt confirming my status. I'm sure the boss found the badge in the street and gave it to me as a sop to my ego and in the forlorn hope I would dress up smarter. He doesn't realize how filthy your clothes can get from kneeling on piss and cum-soaked linoleum or what spunk does when it gets on good shirts and trousers.

With the recession the way it is, punters seem to have given up porn. Sex, no, especially as I'm giving it away for free. Porn, yes. In those days, our biggest seller was the Butthole 3000, the Apple iPad of ass-fuck toys. We couldn't keep up to the demand. As fast as we put 'em out, they got snapped up. Or stolen. In the end we had to keep 'em under lock and key. Some dirty bastards even tested them in the shop while their buddies distracted my attention. I had to sluice them out and try to get them back in their cardboard boxes.

If I'd had any selling nous at all, I probably could have doubled the price and sold them with the slimy deposit still inside. We have one guy comes to the shop, we call him Dyson, cause he spends every spare moment sucking up the cum deposits other guys leave in the booths with glory holes and small porno screens.

But I'm getting off the subject. The secret to the Butthole 3000 was that, one, they were made from this great new synthetic product that so closely resembled real human skin, flesh, and muscle that it was being used for grafts in hospitals. Two, it was so realistic that when one turned up in the harbor, news reports ran amok for a day or two believing there was a killer on the loose who was dismembering his victims. Three, it didn't hurt that it was cast from the ass of the century. That ass belonged to gay porn star and power bottom, Jarvis Poule, star of such notorious masterpieces as *The Curious Case of Benjamin Butt, Beavis and Butt-Hole,* and *Butt Buggers of Planet Porno.* Benjamin Butt is the name he went by when he first entered the business and worked for some of those fly-by-night studios that crank out loops featuring anonymous street trash. He became Jarvis when he was picked up by one of the major gay porn directors who mentored him, signing him to an exclusive contract.

His cock is a respectable seven inches, he works out at the gym every day, his ass is insured for a million bucks, and he's listed in the Guinness Book of records as the man who has taken the most cocks up his ass in one year. The verified tally is 2175, and even then he admits there were a few on the side when the records people had gone home for the day.

How do I know so much about him? Because I love Jarvis Poule, his current screen nom de porn. I even know that his last name is French for pothole. I know also he was born plain old Bobby Tico in Cathedral City, California, and had his heart set on being a brain surgeon until his ultra-conservative dad found him down on his knees with the rector from his local church, not in worship but fellating the old guy in exchange for divine forgiveness and enough cheap altar wine to tie one on.

After that he lived on the streets, selling his ass to stay alive. It's where he learned his butt was his fortune and he's taken good care of it ever since and, in return, it has taken good care of him.

My story really begins the night he made a personal appearance at the store. Nothing to do with promotion. No one knew he was coming, so to speak. But he did. Come, that is. Unfortunately for Dyson, he wasn't there that night to collect some of the most famous sperm in the universe.

I knew it was him as soon as he entered the shop. I expected an entourage to trail after him, but he was alone. Very low key. He was in town to promote his latest movie, *Butt Privates,* and was dancing on a small stage set up in the corner of the bar next door, as well as stripping late at night in a sleazy nearby club where the climax of his act was his own climax which he left slimy and neglected on the worn wooden stage after the audience had the opportunity to paw his body and finger his hole.

You had to pay a premium if you wanted to get that close to the asshole from heaven, a price too rich for my pocket. Those prime positions normally went to middle-aged men with bank balances bigger than their pricks. They all had visions of taming that ass and getting it to settle down. Those guys wanted a trophy, not a lover.

I didn't want him as either. I had big dreams, really big. I wanted to be a superhero like Superman or Green Lantern or one of those dudes. If people asked what superpower I would love above all else if I could only choose one, I never hesitated: I wanted an asshole of steel. You see, if I couldn't be a comic book hero, I wanted to beat Jarvis's record. To that end I kept a sort of unofficial diary of the numbers of men who fucked me. Some mornings it was so busy I couldn't keep count of how many I took in my butt as opposed to those in my mouth or my hand. I did know, however, that even allowing for an error rate of ten per cent I was still trailing Jarvis by thousands.

Sure, I didn't have the opportunities he did, but even with my Sunday morning gangbangs my ass was fuckin' sore after ten to twelve guys. Jarvis had to average around six cocks up his ass every day for a year to achieve his record. I reckoned I could do that easily if I spread them out, but it was finding the guys.

I didn't have all that much of a problem pulling sex partners. I was a jock at college, my body's fit, tanned and gym-toned – I keep it that way to help achieve my personal goal – and I'm fairly good-looking in a straight jock way. There's the problem in a nutshell: gay guys want *me* to fuck *them*. Of course, I will, but that doesn't help me toward my dream. You won't find anyone listed in the record books as having fucked 2175 guys or chicks in a year. The cock's not built for that sort of punishment, but some asses are, mine being one of them.

Jarvis Poule's ass most certainly was. I just wanted to talk to him, tell him how much I admired him and see if I could pick up a few hints as to technique, that sort of shit. The last thing I wanted to be was an unknown or unremembered notch in his ass ring. I can't name a single one of the people who helped Jarvis achieve his record, not even the well-known porno stars who fucked him on screen that year. No one remembered them, least of all Jarvis.

Unfortunately, the night he turned up was one of those occasions in which troublemakers predominated in the shop, those superior yuppies who think the ideal end to a Saturday night is visiting a sex shop to guffaw loudly at the magazines and pretend a worldliness they don't even come close to possessing. I'd just banned two hetero couples for their disruptive behavior. They'd managed to empty the place of regulars with their embarrassing shrieks and their uncouth behavior until they became so obnoxious I threw them out. That made their night and they were heading off to tell their friends they'd been thrown out of a sex shop. Says a lot for their manners; they thought it was hilarious.

Worse were the straight boys in packs showing off to the girlfriends. Worst of all were the straight boy packs showing off to one another. Most of the time they were simply raucous but there was usually an underlying feeling of menace, made more palpable if they were drunk. Occasionally, violence flared but I kept a baseball bat handy in case of trouble, and the police were on speed dial. I also had Chen, a martial arts instructor, who called in most nights after training to watch straight pornos. He'd once saved me from a drug addict who'd attempted to rob me of the night's takings. The would-be thief had been so off his face he couldn't hold the knife steady and was an easy target for Chen who dropped him with a maneuver that neither his victim nor I saw coming.

We didn't bother with the cops, we just carried the poor bugger out onto the street and dumped him in the gutter. Chen was a great looking guy with a slim hairless body that I thought chicks would have gone wild over. I know I did, and tried to get him to fuck me in the beginning. The first time it had been one of those boring nights where nothing was happening. Chen was in one of the porno booths jerking off. I knew that's what he did because I'd received numerous complaints from people who'd stepped in his spooge after he'd done the dirty and vacated the booth.

Dyson loved it when his visits coincided with one of Chen's because he would wait patiently outside the booth until Chen finished, then he would zap inside to siphon the juice off the floor and the wall. I'm keen on cum but there are limits to what I'll do to get it.

That first night I propositioned Chen, I closed and locked the front counter, hung a sign saying 'Back in 10 Mins' and headed back to the booths. I kneeled on the floor to watch him stroking his smooth hard cock, the one I wanted to taste more than anything that night. Although I hissed and invited him to fill my mouth by beckoning with my index finger and my tongue through the glory hole, he ignored me until he was ready to blow. Only then did he turn and aim his cock toward the hole in the wall. Once I realized he was not about to indulge in any sort of penetration whatsoever but was willing to let me have his nut juice, I pasted my lips to that hole, poking my tongue through as his spunk splatted against the wall and into my grateful mouth.

Later, back at the counter, I apologized for distracting him but he shrugged it off. "I wish I could," he said. "But I don't do gay. It doesn't worry me if you want my cum, that's fine, but I won't stick my cock in your mouth."

"There were a couple of complaints about the amount of spooge you shoot when you first started coming here," I told him. "But if I see you're in, I usually just mop it up before anyone else steps in it. Your girlfriend must almost drown in it when you shoot in her mouth."

"She doesn't like my dick in her mouth," he said.

"I think you need a new girlfriend."

"I think so too, but our families…" He crossed two fingers to show how close they were. "It's expected we'll marry."

"Listen, how about I give you a container you can shoot into when you want to watch a porno, which saves on the clean-up," I suggested.

He laughed. "You got a big enough bucket?"

He wasn't kidding. To Dyson's disappointment, Chen left no more nasty deposits in the booth. He would head to the counter when he first arrived and I'd hand him a plastic container with a wide enough mouth that he didn't have to concentrate too hard on aiming and thus reduce the pleasure. He never asked what I did with it, perhaps because he came back to the counter to ask me a question one time and caught me with the container to my lips, swallowing his load. "Nasty," he smiled, never mentioning it again.

In exchange for his generosity I allowed him booth time for free.

Sometimes he'd stop to chat about nothing in particular or would browse the magazines. I'd let him take one away and he'd bring it back a few days later, as good as new and I'd re-bag it and pop it back on the shelf.

He wasn't like some guys who treated me like a bartender, telling me the story of their lives or asking me to solve their personal problems. Those sorts of guys one tires of quickly.

This night there were a couple of all-male bucks night straight groups came through. They were usually pretty harmless, asking about blow-up dolls or cheap sex toys mainly to embarrass the prospective groom. Sometimes they'd ask if I was gay. These guys were usually outer suburban working class kids in their late teens early twenties, amazed that I answered in the affirmative. It was always interesting when one or more of the group asked about the nitty gritty of gay sex because you could be almost guaranteed that guy would be back for a taste of cock sometime in the near future without his mates.

My ass had felt many a straight boy experimenting before he fled back to the safety of his suburban existence. It was the ones who wanted to know what kissing another guy was like that I knew I'd see coming into the shop on a more regular basis. Them I tried to ease into the lifestyle as best I could.

One such group was yahooing around the shelves of Barely Legal and Schoolgirl porn mags. "If she's a schoolgirl, she must have repeated classes for a fuckin' eternity," said the leader of the pack. You could see why he was the alpha male of the group: he was built like a brick shithouse, the bulge in his jeans promised ecstasy, and he was so handsome it made your teeth hurt. The gay guys cruising the magazine aisles hovered perilously close ready to pounce if his gang ever gave them enough wriggle space. I could sense a disaster waiting to happen here.

Then the group moved on to the gay mags and started with the "Oh that's so gross, dude," and "Let's get away from the faggot shit."

That's why I didn't notice Jarvis Poule until he stood in my line of vision and coughed.

"I'm sorry, can I…?"

At that point my eyes met his and my mouth literally dropped open. A buzz had already gone round the gay guys in the store, some of them even coming out from the booths at the back to take a look.

"Three bottles of Head Crush if you have them," he said as I just stood there staring. He must have been used to it because he acted as if there were nothing untoward in my behavior. I'd rehearsed this moment in my mind so many times. Not exactly this moment but one in which I got up close enough to Jarvis Poule to speak to him. I couldn't remember a single line I'd rehearsed, all that wit, all that repartee, all that…shit, I was such a loser.

I extracted the three small bottles from the bar fridge under the counter and went to wrap them in a brown paper bag.

"Don't worry about bagging them, I'll sniff them here."

It was a joke and I smiled accordingly, still tongue-tied. He handed me the cash for his purchase and I gave him change. He leaned over the counter. "You have a beautiful mouth, but you need to close it sometimes and breathe."

I gulped in air, not realizing I'd been holding my breath. I grabbed the counter to stop from falling over.

"The porno booths?" he enquired.

I pointed to the back of the shop.

He turned his most provocative smile on me. "Talkative little thing, aren't you? You must suck a lot of cock."

As he made his way through the aisles the straight boys must have found some of the magazines that featured him because there was a lot of whispering and pointing plus a couple of magazines got passed around. I decided to ignore the fact that they'd ripped one out of its plastic cover and were flipping through the pages obviously in awe of Jarvis's prowess taking cock.

"How is that even possible?" one the gang asked.

There was stunned silence as they went through the pages until they must have reached the spooge shots. A couple of the group screwed their faces up in horror.

"You think he's gonna…" one guy said, nodding toward the magazine. "Out there?"

"Let's go see," the top cocky said, following Jarvis to the booths. Some customers smelled trouble and made a hasty exit, others decided to play follow the straight boys. Expecting problems, I moved the bat closer, flicking the view on the security cameras to the booth area so I could keep an eye on what was happening. The vision was in black and white with no sound but I was an astute observer of body language.

Jarvis went into a booth but left the door ajar which was an open invitation to anyone who wanted to join him. The booths on either side were already occupied, so the straight boys crowded into the one directly opposite. They closed the door and must have decided to watch one of the porno movies on offer because the light above their door went on. That's how I can keep track of who's using the booth for sex without dropping coins in the slot.

I can do the old routine, 'Coins in the slot, please, Booth six,' from the counter via the security set-up.

Jarvis's light went on and I assume he was having a ball or two at the neighboring glory holes. Unfortunately, I couldn't see into the booths themselves but I could imagine. A few men cruising the area stopped to peer into Jarvis's cubicle before moving on, although one of two congregated around the door fascinated by what they were watching. Two of them had their cocks out, stroking as they watched what activity there was to see.

When one of the booths beside Jarvis opened and a young man made his escape, one of the guys jerking off soon elbowed his way in forgetting to latch the door so now there were two booths that attracted a crowd. There was inevitability to the unfolding drama that would have fascinated Tennessee Williams. Sure, there were straight guys around but they just ignored any gay activity if they didn't want to be involved, but the gang was an unknown quantity.

My attention was distracted by customer purchases or men wanting change for the booths and someone who wanted a demonstration of the Butthole 3000. When I told him that Jarvis himself was in one of the booths he rang his buddies to tell them then headed out back himself. When I looked at the screen again, the crowd had swollen to gangbang proportions and men were lining up to enter the booths on either side or else pushing their way into the Jarvis cubicle. Guys were photographing the action on their cell phones and texting.

This was threatening to get out of hand.

I'd have to seal off the booth area to prevent anyone else gaining entrance shortly because it already held more men than the fire department permitted. I so wanted to be part of the crowd if only to watch my hero in action.

There must be a god because no sooner had I sent my wish out into the universe than a guy dragged Jarvis out of the booth, forcing him to his knees in the middle of the mob. Jarvis seemed totally unconcerned by the number of men who wanted a go at his body as he got down in doggy position so one man could penetrate his mouth while another went at his ass.

The guy was gonna be fucked to death except I knew he could take it. The gay men were like sexual locusts feeding on his body but leaving their spooge in their wake. I admit it, I was envious.

The straight guys had totally slipped my mind until I saw their booth door open. Even on the small screen it was obvious they were shocked by the sexual free-for-all. I kept my eye on the leading alpha because the others would take their cue from him although some of the straight boys were already adjusting their cocks in their jeans. I wasn't sure whether that was from watching porn or seeing gay sex live in front of them.

The crush was getting worse; poppers were being passed from hand to hand until even the straight boys were almost off their faces, their cocks hanging out of their jeans waiting a turn. Poppers were also spilled on the floor which must have added to the general confusion, setting libidos on fire in the enclosed space.

I saw Jarvis look to the camera in desperation as he disappeared beneath a sea of cock and cum. I yelled into the PA system, "Okay guys, give him room, and let him breathe. If you don't all behave in an orderly fashion, I'll have to close it down." I could tell the crowd didn't take kindly to my announcement, the pushing and shoving becoming more violent as men wrestled to get at Jarvis in case their access was limited. It was time to act. Grabbing the baseball bat, I headed for the back of the shop and the booth area, slapping the bat against the palm of my hand for emphasis.

The stench of cum, sweat and poppers was so ripe I was amazed it hadn't seeped into the shop and out onto the streets. The guys were obviously off their faces which is why they couldn't see sense. I waded into the melee, pulling and pushing men out of the way until I found Jarvis, flat on his back, his legs over some dude's shoulders as the guy rammed his cock into that insatiable ass. Another poked his cock into my hero's throat, choking him because of the awkward angle. Others, simply too turned on to wait their turn, shot their spunk over his body so that he was slick as an oiled bodybuilder.

I tried to calm them but the odor from the spilled poppers meant they were so turned on they didn't take any notice of my attempt to establish order. In fact, they turned on me. If you've never been in the midst of a stoned mob, high on poppers, eager to get their rocks off then you don't know the fearsome single-mindedness of men. It was terrifying while at the same time deliciously perverse. That was the poppers talking. Yes, even my brain was pounding with the heady aroma that went straight to my cock and ass.

I attempted to prod people away from Jarvis with the bat but that only got them incensed. As I made my way through the wall of bodies to rescue Jarvis, one of my regulars grabbed at me, tearing my scummy old shirt off my back. "Hey, it's the guy from the front counter. Grab him. He loves cock up his ass. Hold him down while I fuck him. His ass is so sweet."

I was close enough to Jarvis to push his assailants to one side. "Get the fuck out of here," I yelled, hoping the lynch mob would calm down when their prey was gone. I pushed a few guys with the bat and Jarvis scrambled through an opening between the bodies. I turned to the crowd, appealing to them to disperse when the bat was yanked from my hand and I felt pain as someone whacked me on the back. I stumbled to the ground, my jeans manhandled off my body, my briefs shredded until I was totally nude apart from my runners.

I disappeared under the quicksand of too many bodies to escape. A yell of 'Fuck him!' rang out and I felt fingers piercing my ass and cocks shoved in my face. This wasn't quite the way I wanted to attempt Jarvis's record, and there were not thousands surrounding me but a couple of dozen, so it was best that I relax and hope that my idol had gone for help.

"Hey guys," someone yelled. "The bar fridge under the front counter is full of poppers. Here."

Now I was in deep shit, they'd broken into the booth behind the counter. If they'd found the drugs, they'd probably prized open the till and stolen the night's takings as well.

My ass was savagely fingered to open me up for the cocks that were dribbling in anticipation. This wasn't about fucking Jarvis, the anal superstar. This was just about getting your cock in a hole. Any hole. I had expected the crowd would turn on one another but they seemed united in treating one person as a fuck hole cum dump. It had begun as Jarvis, it was now me. I didn't struggle in case they turned violent, I did my best to lie back and enjoy it.

The guy who'd raided the fridge for poppers opened a few bottles, sprinkling the contents on the floor so the vapors erupted all around, making our hearts pulse, the oxygen pumping through our systems, breaking down barriers. I would have a fuckin' terrible headache in the morning. Hell, I'd have a sphincter muscle like a stretched elastic band and a mouth that tasted like a used asshole. If I survived. It did worry me that the guys seemed intent on causing as much damage and pain as they could when they took a turn.

My ass had been breached and cock after cock pounded into me until they blew their sloppy load caking my ass tunnel with spunk until it began to dribble from my butthole. My mouth received equal punishment, my oxygen blocked so often I thought I would pass out.

I was surrounded by snarling sex-crazed animals shoving not only fingers and cocks up my ass, but also attempting to get their fists inside me and anything to hand such as dildos and even the baseball bat. I was choked, called all the filthy names the guys could hurl from their unleashed sexual depravity. Even the leader of the straight pack eventually wedged his blunt prick in my guts, spitting his contempt by calling me 'faggot' while his buddies all egged him on, jerking their own cocks in my face until I was almost smothered with globs of their thick, warm spooge.

I called out for help but it went unheard. I felt my asshole being stretched by something painful and splintery. I screamed once and passed out.

"Mr. Rogers," A voice called. "Mr. Rogers, wake up."

I didn't want to wake up. I tried to mumble to the voice to go away and leave me alone but my throat was full of phlegm. I tried to clear it but then I discovered a tube.

I sat up suddenly, crying, "The pain."

I heard footsteps across the floor, then a needle prick and I slipped back into oblivion.

The next time I awoke, I knew I was in a hospital from the buzz of activity around me, the beep of machines, the smell of disinfectant and illness making me sneeze.

A nurse stood at the end of my bed consulting a chart. She must have seem my eyelids flutter open because she said, "You're awake, Mr. Rogers."

I thought that was bloody obvious but I didn't say so. Instead, I groaned.

"Are you in pain?"

I nodded my head.

"The doctor prescribed pain medication and it's been some time since your last dose, so I don't see the harm."

I felt like saying, "I love you" when she administered the injection but instead I sank down into a gooey warmth that enveloped me like an old friend. I felt safe there. No one could harm me.

I spent long days and nights living like a spermatozoon in a sea of seminal fluid before my head cleared and the pain was little more than a dull throb. A nurse plumped up my pillows and helped me sit up. When she lifted the sheet and blanket to cover me I almost screamed.

"What's that?" I pointed.

"We have to drain your waste out somehow, Mr. Rogers," she said not unreasonably.

"What happened to me?"

"You don't know?"

"Last thing I remember…oh, fuck!"

"Oh, fuck, is right," she smiled.

"How did I get here?"

"Your friends called an ambulance. And the police. They had to break it up, although from what I hear some of them were overcome by the fumes and started to join in. We treated them here. That's not the official version, however."

"Does everyone in the hospital know about what happened to me?"

She tucked the blanket under the mattress successfully trapping me in the bed. "You're famous, Mr. Rogers."

"What? There were more than 2175 of them? No wonder I'm in hospital."

She didn't get the joke so I let it lie. But I didn't get why I was famous.

"The doctor will explain when he gets here. I've called him and he's keen to talk to you."

I lay back against the pillow, exhausted from just the small exertion of conversation. I couldn't remember much of that fateful night except the hungry faces looming over me and the thrusting, thrusting, thrusting at my mouth and ass. I ran my hand under the sheet to my ass but I was wearing a giant adult diaper. That couldn't be good.

"What day is it?" I asked.

When the nurse told me, I calculated that I'd been in and out of consciousness for almost a week.

Dr. Brewer was a silver fox, he could do me any time. Well, maybe not right now, but I was glad to see that my libido hadn't suffered.

"How are you feeling, Mr. Rogers?"

Why do they always ask that? Does anyone ever feel chipper when they wake up in hospital?

"What happened to me?"

"You're lucky to be alive, Mr. Rogers."

So it is possible to be fucked to death.

"Please, call me Henry."

"Well, Henry, you lost a lot of blood. You were in a pretty bad state when you were brought in. The paramedics thought they'd lost you at one stage."

Lost me? He made it sound like I'd gone walkabout in a suburban shopping center rather than had a near-death experience.

"But they brought you back and, well, here you are."

I couldn't help the sarcasm. "As far as stories go, it seems to be lacking a little detail. Care to color it in?"

The doctor smiled. "Sarcasm is good, Henry. As far as details about what happened, the police will want to interview you as soon as I give the okay. The most I can tell you is that someone attempted to insert an object in your rectum that had a small nail attached. It ripped your anal lining open, you lost a lot of blood and…well, let's not dwell on the unpleasant aspects."

I dreaded what my next question would reveal. "Is that why I have the bag? My ass is stitched up?"

"That was our first intention. The simplest expedient, as well as being the cheapest, was to give you a colostomy bag. But your friend, Mr. Poule, convinced us that…um…how can I put this?"

He hesitated for so long, I felt I had to fill in the blanks. "He told you I take it up the ass and I wouldn't be too pleased to wake up to discover the entrance shut and bolted."

"You certainly have a way with words, Henry."

"So, am I or aren't I?"

"Your friend, Mr. Poule, can be very persuasive. I was brought in because a few of us here have been experimenting with using a new polymer for burns and various other injuries. When Mr. Poule showed us the…ah…Butthole 3000, it gave me an idea. You were in and out of consciousness and, quite frankly, we didn't expect you to live, so I thought, why the hell not?"

"I was a guinea pig?"

Dr. Brewer corrected me gently. "You were a pioneer in medical research. Henry, you don't realize, if this operation is successful, it will be a great step forward for medical science. For people with burns, with scarring. It will even help gender reassignments."

"Wait. Are you telling me you've transplanted a Butthole 3000 into my ass?"

"You put it crudely, yes, that's essentially what we did."

I was delighted. "I have Jarvis Poule's asshole."

The doctor smiled. "You could put it that way, I suppose. I did a little research. I had no idea he was so famous."

"Does my new asshole work?"

"We don't know yet. We won't be able to tell until we close the stoma and you revert to natural excretion."

"When will that be?"

"There are a few tests we'd like to run and I can't see any reason why it can't be quite soon."

"Will I be able to feel anything?"

I dreaded that I'd get my ass back, for which I would be more than grateful, but not the feeling to go with it.

"We're hopeful, but we're not sure."

"The nurse said something about me being famous…"

He reddened as if the nurse should not have mentioned the subject. "Well…ah…the newspapers got hold of the story." He stopped. "Look, you know what tabloid journalism is like. They dubbed you The Six Million Dollar Asshole." I must have looked stricken because he said, "No, it didn't cost anywhere near that much although it was expensive. The costs have been covered so don't go getting depressed. You need to keep your spirits up." He rose to leave. "By the way, I did like one name that a newspaper bestowed on you. It has a heroic ring to it."

I dreaded to ask.

"They called you Butt Rogers. Quite clever, don't you think?"

After I pondered it for a while, I did agree that it was clever.

The next week was a flurry of tests and visits from specialists who wanted to examine the guinea pig for themselves. I think I had my asshole prodded more in that week than I had in the months leading up to my hospitalization excluding, of course, that eventful night.

The police also called in to interview me but they could tell me little more than I had been attacked by a band of thugs who had caused the injury and ransacked the shop. I was found by a Mr. Jarvis Poule and a Mr. Chen Yu who called paramedics and the police. If they had not arrived on the scene when they did, it seems there was a very strong chance I would have bled to death.

There was no CCTV footage of the assault because the shop had security cameras but no facility for recording. That was a godsend, I suppose, although I would have liked to know the identity of the bastard who did this to me.

I was surprised during that second week by a visitor.

"Knock, knock," he said as he stood in the doorway.

It was none other than Jarvis Poule himself, with an enormous bunch of flowers, which he presented to me with a blush of embarrassment.

"They said you were well enough to receive visitors," he explained. "I was out of town for a shoot so this is the first opportunity I've had." He leaned over and kissed me on the cheek.

It was almost worth enduring all the pain and discomfort just for that.

"I owe you my life," I said. "Thank you."

"It's I who should be thanking you," he corrected. "If you hadn't stepped in when you did, it would have been me on the receiving end of that jagged nail." He shuddered at the thought.

"I really do appreciate all you've done for me," I said.

He squeezed my hand.

"If it hadn't been for me wanting to fill in time between gigs…"

"Thanks for making up that story about the thugs. I don't think anyone would have believed the truth."

"You're welcome. But, you know, it was Chen who got rid of the crowd. I yelled that the cops were on their way but a few of them didn't want to leave without, well, you know, even though there was blood everywhere. He's pretty good with his fists and his feet. Pity he's straight."

"Tell me about it," I replied, though I did take Jarvis into my confidence concerning the plastic containers of spooge.

"You nasty bitch," he screamed with delight.

It turned out Jarvis's visit was just the cheer-up I needed. We shrieked so much it attracted the nurses, some of the males recognizing my visitor and crowding him for autographs. When we were left alone again, he said, "Well, come on, show me."

"Show you what?"

"My asshole sewn into your butt."

"I hear I have you to thank for that."

"I didn't think you'd really want your vital assets sewn up at such a young age. It seemed the most practical solution. Did it work?"

"The doctors don't know yet, they're conducting tests."

"Oh those doctors," he huffed. "The best test is between their legs, honey. Get you up on your hands and knees and slam a good hard cock up your plastic ass and see if you yelp."

"I think they'd be struck off if they tried that," I laughed. For a moment I did wonder what it would be like to have the most famous bottom in the world stick his cock inside me. I let the idea go.

"Your cock still works, right?" Jarvis didn't give me time to answer, he just reached under the blanket to squeeze my cock which had been rock hard since he made his entrance. "My, you are a big boy."

Before I could stop him, his head joined his hand under the bedclothes and his warm mouth clamped down around my cock. Oh God, the feeling was so good. I didn't know if I could come but I allowed Jarvis to continue working his magic on me so I could memorize his technique. We were interrupted before he could complete his task but it didn't matter. I'd had Jarvis Poule's lips around my cock. My hero had sucked me. Considering he'd gone down on countless thousands of men before, it was no big deal, except to me who never expected anything like that to happen.

He visited every few days, keeping me up to date on gossip, generally just making me laugh, even through the painful times when the surgeons rerouted my bowels so I could take my first shit since the injury. Because I had a plastic anal pussy now I expected to feel nothing. Boy was I wrong. I think they heard my screams on the moon.

I'd practiced dilating my sphincter with a vibrator the hospital supplied just to get me used to the feeling. The bloody thing was smaller than any cock I'd taken so I had to ask Jarvis to bring me something more appropriate next time he called.

To my surprise, Chen dropped by to update me on the sex shop which he now avoided as the new night staff were drug pushers and assholes. He was very sweet and brought me a plastic container with a lid. "My mother won't miss it," he said as he handed it to me shyly. "I filled it up in the toilet just before I came to your room."

Not wishing his mother to go without one of her plastic containers for too long, I quaffed the warm slime in front of him, licking the insides to get every last drop. It had been so long since I'd had a cock or cum. I didn't class the doctor's prodding my new rectum as proper sex although I did manage an erection on a few occasions while he was examining me.

Jarvis was a godsend. He brought just the right size dildo with him the next time he came. "Get this in your ass sweetie and you're well on the road to recovery. You sure you should be doing this?"

I was eager to get out of hospital so the sooner I practiced with something closer to what I was used to the easier it would be.

Jarvis locked the door. "Get up on your hands and knees honey so I can grease that butt hole of yours."

I did as I was told, gritting my teeth in determination. Jarvis lathered my ass liberally with lubrication, pushing a finger in slowly until the pain subsided. He was a caring conspirator. He managed to get three fingers inside me although not as deep as a cock would have gone. It was time.

"Okay, use the dildo on me but take it very slowly. One, because I don't want it to bust me open and, two, because I want to see if I can feel it inside me."

I buried my face in the bedclothes as he propped the pillows under me for support.

"I would have brought poppers, but under the circumstances…"

I laughed, wondering whether it might have helped when I took my first shit through my new ass.

"I wonder what your new ass tastes like?" he asked as I felt him slap the rubber dildo against my butt cheeks.

"Help yourself," I laughed.

"Maybe next time before your hole is all slick with lube," he said.

I felt the head of the dildo against my ring. I tensed. I couldn't help it.

"Relax, honey. Tell me if it hurts and I'll pull it out right away. Okay."

He massaged my back as he began to push the dildo between the folds of my sphincter. That, I could very definitely feel. He continued by pushing in and then pulling out, a slow stabbing motion that was doing my head in because I wanted the full feeling in my bowels, but I knew better than to back up on it suddenly.

His perseverance paid off. I took deep breaths as he pushed, willing myself to relax. It seemed to take ages but eventually the head of the dildo broke through and was embedded in my ass.

"That feels so damn good," I moaned. "Keep going."

I knew the doctor would never have done this for me, I was glad Jarvis had agreed. The guy had become a really close friend. He was more than a hero to me now, he was my lifeline to the future.

Millimeter by millimeter the dildo slid in until my own cock was rock hard leaking pre-cum. I wanted to jerk off but I knew that once I came I wouldn't be able to stand the pressure in my ass. I had to hold off, no matter how turned on I was.

"Honey, it's almost all the way in. All seven inches of it," Jarvis said in wonder. "How's it feel."

"Fuckin' wonderful," I replied. "Fuck me gently with it so I can see how much feeling I've got. The doc said it would come back slowly."

"Okay, but tell me if it hurts."

"You can bet your ass, I will."

It did feel wonderful as the rubber cock pushed in and pulled out slowly, going deeper, deeper until I felt the scratchy pubes and the balls against my butt.

Pubes? Balls?

"What the fuck, Jarvis?"

"You are so fuckin' tight, dude," he said, as I turned my head as far as it would go to see it was his cock buried to the hilt up my ass. "I hope you realize I don't do this for just anybody. This is our little secret, I don't want it getting out that I top as good as I bottom."

"Keep fucking me like that and I won't breathe a word of it," I agreed.

"Why don't you lie on your back so mama can watch your face as I fuck your cute little ass? I better watch you, you could be competition."

Jarvis pulled out and I lay on my back as he very gingerly raised my legs to place them on his shoulders. His cock went deeper this time and I felt him hit my prostate, sending stars through my brain.

"You sure are a cute fucker," he said. "I love that look you get on your face when I sink real deep inside your ass, making you my bitch."

"I'll be your bitch any time," I admitted. "Just keep fucking me like that."

I love being fucked hard but this wasn't the occasion, although Jarvis did pick up speed toward the end. He plugged my mouth with his tongue as his cock expanded and shot wads of spunk deep inside me.

"I swear, man, if you were a chick, you'd be pregnant now."

I believed him because I could feel his love juice leaking out of me as he pulled his cock out. He wasn't finished by a long shot. He nuzzled my balls before running his tongue up my shaft then swallowing me down his tight throat. He gave a first class porn star performance guzzling my prick until I couldn't hold off any longer and I fed him my load. He smacked his lips theatrically, "Sweet."

Of course, as fate would have it, that was the afternoon the doctor decided to have a look at my asshole. Jarvis sat in a corner trying not to snicker as the doc examined my rectum which was spilling spooge around his gloved finger. "I see you've had some help practicing. Mind telling me how it was?"

At least he had a sense of humor. When he'd finished the examination, he told me I could keep practicing like that if I liked but to keep a note of any change in the feelings. With luck I'd be going home in a matter of days.

Home?

I didn't have a home. Jarvis had taken care of putting my small amount of furniture and my collection of comics in storage. No job, no rent money. If I wanted severance pay, I'd have to sue the owners of the sex shop. It wasn't worth the hassle, plus I suspected the owners names were hidden under a mountain of false paper trails that it would take years to unravel.

"Hey, don't stress," Jarvis said. "You can come live with me until you get back on your feet. I've got plenty of room."

I stifled a sob of gratitude.

"Hey, enough of that," he said, wiping the damp from under my eye with his thumb. "You need to practice. Isn't that what the doc said?"

I nodded.

"And wasn't that cock the perfect fit to practice with?"

I nodded again.

"Well, there's only one of it in the entire world and I ain't parting with it for anybody, so doesn't it make sense that you move in with my cock so you can practice any time you want, day or night?"

"I guess. What if my cock needs a bit of practice from time to time?"

"Oh, I think I can definitely accommodate that."

Being realistic, though, my ass would take time to heal and the doctor advised to dilate as frequently as possible.

"You sure you're up for all this...practice?"

"Definitely," Jarvis said, kissing me on the mouth. "Who knows? It could lead to a whole new career for me as a top."

K-POP TARTS

The two stalkers stood watching, offering comments that were in danger of turning me off my allotted task.

"Fuck me!" the man below me screamed. "Get your cock inside me now!"

He was not to be disobeyed. He could have my nuts for garters, my job, my whole career, if I didn't obey him. That was my excuse. I tucked thoughts of my boyfriend back home to one side and concentrated on the hot man beneath me, his legs spread apart revealing his puckered purple hole that dribbled lubrication and the remnants of the earlier fuck. I positioned the throbbing head of my prick at his entrance; it looked much too small to take my cock.

"Don't do it, dude." Bi-ho warned. "You'll tear him apart with that monster."

"Come on," Ha-joon said, cringing as I pushed ever-so-gently against my prey's sphincter. "He'll rip you apart."

"Shut the fuck up," the subject of all this pseudo concern screamed. Turning to me, he demanded, "Give it to me hard."

I slammed my meat into the tightest, warmest asshole I'd ever fucked. I groaned as his ass muscles clenched around my cock, his breath hissing between his teeth as the pain stabbed home, his mates cringing as his hole stretched to the limit to accommodate my girth.

He'd placed his hands on my thighs to signal he needed time to adjust to the fullness in his butt. I watched as he tentatively withdrew one hand, then the other. He looked into my eyes dreamily as I began to saw my cock gently in and out of his ass. I would get much rougher later.

He burbled his satisfaction, then asked, "Why don't you ring your vampire boyfriend?"

* * * *

There were fuckin' people everywhere; jabbering at me, poking me, pushing me, demanding this and that, asking directions. I could only image what it must be like outside the venue. Here inside, it was bedlam. I was expected to be nanny, nursemaid, therapist, lost and found, as well as confidence booster. I'd never come across so many fragile egos. On the plus side I'd never come across so many hot fuckin' men. My cock was permanently hard even though most of them were out of my league, especially the boy bands, those cute young twinks, all legal mind although no one seemed to be over about twenty-three. They wouldn't even give me a second look. Security was always taken for granted until something went wrong. Then all the shit and the blame are heaped on us.

I can take it. I have broad shoulders. I'm a huge fucker – you gotta be in this profession. In fact, I'm probably intimidating to those cute twinks I tower over. I could crush an entire boy band in one hand or bounce them on my bicep, smother them between my pecs. I'm not muscle bound, and I don't do steroids, but I'm fuckin' ripped. Ripped enough that I've had my ass patted and my package squeezed several times in tonight's melee. Never managed to make out who it was though in the crush. I hoped it was male.

Didn't matter, my cock wasn't likely to see any action tonight. Speaking of cock, that's where I get my name: Vlad the Impaler. Real name: Vladimir Zeklos. I've Romanian blood coursing through my veins courtesy of my parents, and my dick is as big as the stake they drove through Dracula's dead heart. I'm no vampire though. Just an ordinary, everyday security guard.

It's only after I unzip and haul out my Romanian sausage that I become truly extraordinary. Trouble is, my prick is so long and thick it's hard to find a good man to take it all. Before I met my lover I was constantly frustrated by men whose fantasies were bigger than their mouths or their assholes. I reduced a few of them to quivering terror just by unzipping. Others were reduced to tears after I'd managed to wedge an inch or two into their less than elastic assholes. They all, without exception, pleaded a suddenly remembered prior engagement and fled my bedroom or the steam room or the back alley. Then there were the few who could take me. I loved those guys. Until I met Blake. His ass and his mouth, well, they just fit around my dick like they were meant for each other. To me, that's love.

So, how did I come to find myself so far from home? Blake's an actor. A good one. It's not just me that thinks so. Okay, so his career started in one of those soaps on TV, but it was the most watched thing in the entire history of the world. Maybe a slight exaggeration, but only slight. Hell, I'm biased. His show was popular and I had all the DVDs to prove it. We just hit it off when we met and now we're inseparable. Sigh. Practically inseparable.

Blake wanted the legitimacy of movies so when he was offered the lead role in a romantic comedy with one of the world's top actresses, he jumped at the chance. Bye, bye Blake. No, we didn't split up. He invited me along but I'd once spent a day on the set of his TV series. B-O-R-I-N-G. Not helped by the fact I couldn't spend time with my man. When he wasn't needed for the shoot, he had a script to learn, interviews to endure, and rehearsals to attend. He didn't need me around for any of that. He would have found standing around while I was on the job as security even more tedious.

Also it didn't help that his film was going to be shot on location in a remote country town before moving to the city. No thanks, I'll stay at home. Besides, I had to pay my way; I couldn't allow Blake to pay for everything. Self-respect is important to me.

When this job working as part of a crack security team in Korea was offered, I jumped at the opportunity. The money was very good and it seemed like an easy gig. How wrong I was. I discussed the offer with Blake and as it coincided with his location shoot, we agreed I should take it. He was fuckin' envious as hell; that tickled me. Normally, I'm the one who gets those pangs because he's in such close proximity to the best looking dudes in the world while I'm usually in close proximity to vomit and foul-mouthed bogans who think they can take me on while they spew their guts up outside a club. That's just the women.

This job had me bang in the center of a wet dream. I was one of the security team responsible for maintaining order at the largest festival of Korean Pop,

K-pop to its adherents, in the world. Blake was one of those people from the West who'd been an admirer long before the world-wide phenomena of PSY's "Gangnam Style." He had his favorites and many of them were performing at the concert. I had strict instructions to get autographs. Blake is just a kid at heart.

I was especially instructed to use every means available to get a photo, preferably autographed, of Korea's number one boy band, NQB8, and especially its leader singer, the charismatic but aloof, Q-Dong. He rarely consented to appear on these sorts of multi-talent events preferring his own boy band gigs. He never gave interviews; his autograph was so rare it sold for thousands of dollars on eBay when it was authenticated; and the paparazzi had never managed to capture a shot of him either in public or in private. His appearance at the Rock Asia event was such big news that it meant we had to be extra alert for trouble or anyone getting 'over emotional,' security speak for pissed and aggressive.

Security had been flown in from all over the world because the local firms were seen to be too close to some of the talent or else too open to corruption by the press. Huge sums had been known to change hands for exclusive access to some of the more reticent talent on the roster. I didn't believe for a moment the westerner security guys were any less corruptible than their Korean counterparts so we were rotated in our positions.

It was a three-day event so I spent the first night at the front of the airport-hangar sized auditorium, arms folded, sunglasses perched on my nose so the audience couldn't see where I was looking, attempting to appear as imposing as a muscle mountain. Me and my mates were there to prevent any young female or male from catapulting themselves onto the stage for a quick cuddle with their favorite. It was hot, it was deafening, and it was boring, especially as we couldn't see the performance except in the reflection of absolute adulation in the fans' eyes.

The second night I was one of those chosen to guard the entrances to the building. The side doors were particularly vulnerable to penetration by strangers. When we weren't patrolling the fire doors or the stage door, we were at the glass entrance doors searching bags for weapons and alcohol. We usually turned a blind eye to party drugs because the concert was an endurance test and a few of the security guys were not likely to make it without a little artificial stimulus either.

I don't know whether it was my sheer size or my sparkling personality – I'll vote for number one – that had me picked for backstage duty on the final night. It was my job to keep the more belligerent contestants apart – it was supposed to be politics free but that was sometimes hard to achieve – and to prevent an all-out invasion backstage of horny and star-struck fans. On the second night, hoards of invading fans of both sexes had attempted to crash the Green Room. Only a concerted effort by security prevented a mass assault. A few mates ended up requiring medical assistance. The local press took up the chant about 'western brutality' because an even larger number of fans required hospitalization.

My placid nature was one of the reasons I was chosen for internal security on the final night when NQB8 was to make its appearance. What's more, I was assigned the backstage area that included their dressing room. I'd already collected a number of signed photographs for Blake and made friends with a number of management types hoping they might use me for security in the future. I was friendly without being obtrusive and a few of the guys in the bands who spoke English seemed happy to speak to me in passing.

Not so, Mr. aloof and elusive, Q-Dong. He must have sneaked in via a back entrance before fans began gathering because he was in his dressing room with his back-up singers when I knocked to ensure everything was okay. Not that I got to see him in person. I had to assume the guy who answered my knock was telling the truth. It was my ass if the night's highlight didn't show.

Nerves were wound tight backstage and I was on the receiving end when things went wrong, not that any of it was my job but I understood the temperament of artists, even if half the guys were shit and would be forgotten by the following year. It's a truism, the more mediocre the talent, the more demanding. Most of the gripes were easily fixed by a quick call via my radio mike. A few of the divas were even polite enough to seek me out to apologize for their unreasonable behavior. Them I liked.

As the evening progressed toward the inevitable melee of the concert – they'd only managed sound and lighting checks so far – I could feel exhaustion coming on. I carried a little medicine cabinet in my fanny pack so I managed to pinch a five-minute break to lock myself in one of the men's toilets. It was like an oasis of calm although interrupted by the Tannoy requesting such and such a group onstage for their checks.

I emptied my fanny pack on the imitation marble surrounds of the wash basin after I'd swabbed it clean with the antiseptic wet tissues I always carried with me. I opened the snap-lock plastic bag and chose one of the little white rocket-shaped medicinal's before lowering my tight security trousers and my briefs, allowing my cock to breathe. I had been hard all day while I was surrounded by gorgeous semi-naked twinks, many of whom I would have loved up my ass or buried on the end of my cock. I'd probably have time to relieve the pressure if I hurried. I spat in my palm and began to spread the saliva along my shaft to give me a smooth slick grip as I jerked myself toward nirvana. I sucked the middle finger of my free hand, getting it nice and wet, bypassing my aching balls to press it against my pliable hole. I'd had enough tongues, fingers, and cocks up there that it was not exactly tight as Fort Knox. It wasn't as loose as the Grand Canyon, either.

Pushing the muscle apart without pain, I opened myself up as I jerked my cock faster. I picked up the suppository and pushed it between my sphincter folds until it was way up inside me. In no time at all, I knew my fatigue would be gone and I'd be feeling no pain. In fact, I'd be buzzing for the next twenty-four hours. As a consequence, I'd sleep like a baby on the flight home. I carried all sorts of pills and potions for most occasions, speed being an essential, although I didn't carry or peddle hard drugs.

The odor of sex filled my nostrils as I tugged myself toward orgasm. The fantasies of me and a dozen K-pop boy band members in all sorts of impossible positions propelling me toward the inevitable. I felt no guilt about not including Blake in the free-for-all. This was my fantasy, it wasn't real life. It wasn't cheating.

The Tannoy interrupted what promised to be a volcanic eruption from my balls. "Security to dressing room A6. Repeat. Security to A6."

That was my stretch of corridor. Orgasm would have to wait. Had it been any other dressing room I would have been in no hurry, but that designation belonged to NQB8. If there was a problem, it was my neck in the noose.

I crammed my swollen cock back in my briefs, being careful to zip the fly on my trousers so the shaft didn't get caught in the zipper teeth, and attempted to hide the obscene bulge without success. Oh well, too bad. Hurrying along the maze of corridors, all-too-aware of the smirks, shocks and lip smacking when people saw the front of my trousers, I made it to A6 in record time.

The door was opened to my nervous knock by a distressed young male PA. He ushered me in once I'd shown him my ID tag. When the door closed behind me, the PA turned. In between my entry and the moment that he spoke I'd had a quick look around the dressing room. All was as it should be except for one slight problem: Q-Dong, whom I recognized from his television performances, was crumpled, fetus-like, in a corner of the room, his arms sheltering his face as if attempting to hide from the light.

The PA glared at me accusingly. "This is precisely what you were meant to prevent."

I kept my temper even though I dearly would have loved to grab the assistant by the throat and crush his windpipe. In a situation like this, belligerence didn't help.

Keeping my tone even, bleaching it of any sarcasm, I said, "What precisely is it I'm meant to prevent?"

"That," the PA insisted, pointing his finger at the quivering Q-Dong.

"I can see that Q-Dong needs help, but what precisely is the problem?"

The PA pointed again. "What sort of idiot are you? Can't you use your eyes?"

Still calmly, I replied. "I'm the sort of idiot that will break your finger if you continue to point at an obviously distressed human being and keep shouting 'that' as if it's self-explanatory."

The members of the band who had been tittering and whispering behind their hands stopped to stare at my temerity. Even Q-Dong peeked at me from under his arm.

"I'll have your job for that," the PA spluttered. "No one speaks to me like that and gets away with it."

"Please. Here. Take my job." I unclipped my ID and thrust it in his hand. "If you think you can do it better, then don't let me stop you. It's been fun. However, it might make things easier if next time someone asks you what the problem is, you be a little more forthcoming than just pointing. Understand?"

I was out the door before the PA even had time to react. I slowed my stride along the corridor giving the obnoxious guy a chance. I'd counted to nine before I heard him running after me.

"Security!"

I turned to his ashen face as he caught up to me. "Please."

I merely waited. It was a competition of wills. Finally, he sighed and capitulated. I held the upper hand, after all. He held out his hand. "I'm sorry. My only excuse is that I'm so tense I feel like I'm about to burst."

His grip was strong. I looked at him more closely. Attractive in that young pretty Korean manner. I held his hand longer than necessary but he made no effort to break away. The only hint he knew what I might be thinking was the crimson tide of embarrassment that was rising from his throat.

"Accepted. Let's see what we can do."

As we walked back to the dressing room, the PA explained. "Q-Dong has been getting these threatening text messages from the two men who run his fan club. They've been banned from backstage but…well, that hasn't stopped the threats."

"First thing to do is confiscate his cell phone."

"He won't allow it."

I smiled. "We need to show him who's boss."

Back in the dressing room, Q-Dong was at least now seated at the mirror attempting to get himself ready for the performance. He tried for a few moments and then his head slid forward, banging against the bench.

"Show me these threats," I said.

The PA prized the cell phone from Q-Dong's fingers. I flicked through his messages – he seemed to be very popular – until I found the names of the two guys who ran his unofficial fan club. I laughed at their messages. Most of them were pictures of their, I must say, extremely impressive pricks with offers to stick them in parts of Q-Dong's anatomy where the sun don't shine.

I read through a few more of their texts but they were much of a muchness. "Is there anything more serious than these feeble attempts to fuck you?"

"Isn't that enough?" the PA said.

"If you're not too confident in your masculinity, probably." I turned to Q-Dong. "You feel threatened?"

"Um…no. I think it's funny, but…"

"You're flattered. Just like these other pictures on here of girls who send photos of their tits and their pussies?"

"I guess."

"But Mr. Panic here wants to blow it up out of proportion."

The PA took exception.

"I have such a headache," Q-Dong cried. "I won't be able to perform."

"See what you've done," the PA shouted, rushing to the diva's side, massaging his head gently.

"Okay, here's what we'll do," I said, pushing the PA toward the door. "You go find a spare dressing room and move the rest of the band to it. Leave me here with Q-Dong. I'll find out where these two exhibitionists are seated and have a word with them. Get them to back off. Then, I'll get Q-Dong onto the stage in time for his set. Guaranteed."

The PA was skeptical. "How can you guarantee that?"

I smiled sweetly. "He'll be there even if I have to carry him on myself."

Q-Dong reached for the security of his cell phone. I snapped it closed and stowed it in my pocket. "You can have it back after the show."

When he didn't complain or attempt to grab it back off me, I realized he was pliable and was probably sicker than I had thought at first. When the two of us were alone I stood behind the singer, my heavy hands on his shoulders as he looked at his reflection in the mirror, his face a mask of misery. I kneaded gently and felt the tension in his body.

"You get these headaches often?"

"Much too often," he said in impeccable English. I knew from Blake's adulation that Q-Dong had been educated in England but had been seduced by the pop scene there. He ran foul of a racist recording industry that saw his future in a niche market. He returned to Seoul where he formed his own boy band, to his family's disgust, and had catapulted to local success shortly thereafter based on his good looks, honed body, and remarkable singing ability. The Asian market fell for his prodigious charm and talent within a year and he was currently making inroads in the Australian, north American and European markets.

Q-Dong began to relax under my kneading. My powerful fingers slowly untying the knots in his shoulders before moving to his neck. I'd dimmed the lights, ensuring the room was as quiet as could be in order to build a safe and warm cocoon around the singer. He seemed to be reacting well so far.

"That feels good," he croaked, staring at me in the mirror. "Is this part of your duties?"

I smiled. "Nah, this is a sort of thank you for all your music."

He seemed skeptical. "You know my work? Which is your favorite?"

Anyone could have rattled off the names of one or two of his recent chart successes, so I went for broke, mentioning a number of more obscure songs that only a true aficionado would know.

"You have done your homework well," he smiled. "What did you think of the film clip that goes with 'Under the Cape'? I think it's one of my best."

"It's the only NQB8 song that doesn't have a film clip to accompany it," I said, neatly avoiding the trap he'd set for me. "If you'd had one, I'm sure it would have been a bigger success."

From that moment, we were instant buddies – at least for as long as the concert lasted. I expected no more than that. We were both here to do a job and I knew I was as good at mine as he was with his.

"Why don't you strip down to your briefs and I'll give you a good rubdown? It will get rid of that headache of yours."

"You have magic fingers, Mr. Vlad, but they will not rid me of this migraine. I won't be performing tonight." Nevertheless, he began to disrobe until he was covered only by his briefs.

I placed one of the larger towels along the commodious bench top, inviting Q-Dong to lie face down. Shrugging his indifference, he climbed up and slumped on the plump cotton towel, his face turned toward the mirror as he watched me. Having stowed my backpack in the dressing room earlier – it goes wherever I go as it's loaded with emergency supplies – I retrieved the baby oil, squirting a generous amount onto the palm of my hand before warming it up then spreading it over Q-Dong's shoulders and muscular arms. The guy was a real cutie. My cock throbbed so hard I had to keep it pressed against the bench top in case the singer saw it and freaked. For the moment, at least, it was below his sight line in the mirror.

I worked on him, smoothing out the kinks in his muscles until he was putty in my hands. I got him to turn over, placing a discreet towel across his groin and went to work on his chest, sorely tempted to lean down and gnaw on his pert brown nipples. It felt wonderful to rub my hands across the ridges of his abs and it took a conscious effort of my part not to slip my hand beneath the towel to grasp his cock which I saw twitch as a result of my ministrations. I knew most men, straight as well as gay, were turned on by massage and I wasn't vain enough to take his excitement as an indication of his desire for me.

"Feel any better?"

I helped him sit up, toweling much of the oil off his body. After stretching his neck, he put a finger to his temple. "Still hurts here."

He stood up and almost immediately swayed so precariously I caught him before he fell, helping him across the room to the divan.

"I won't be able to go on."

"Vision blurry?"

"Uh huh."

"I think I've got just the thing. Roll over on your stomach."

His startled expression revealed he still didn't trust me totally. I stood my ground. "Do you want to go on stage tonight?"

He answered with such vehemence I didn't doubt him for a minute. "Of course I do."

"In that case, you'll have to trust me. Okay?"

I could see him thinking. Without a word, he turned over, leaving himself vulnerable to a man who could easily snap his neck with his little finger.

I retrieved my medicine bag from my backpack. Q-Dong looked so delicious lying along the divan I wished Blake could be here to witness it. I didn't dare take a picture with my cell phone because it would be such a betrayal of trust. Kneeling over his thighs I spoke soothingly to him. "This will make the pain go away. You'll feel good after a nap and go onstage to perform better than you ever have before."

My words were hypnotic and suggestive. I kept my voice low and masculine. "I'm going to pull down your underpants now." I felt him flinch beneath me. "There's nothing to worry about. I'm going to massage your butt cheeks and then I'm going to make you feel really, really good."

I slowly peeled his briefs down over his beautiful ass wanting nothing more than to bury my face in his inviting crevice, shoving my nose and tongue at his moist hole like a pig snuffling for truffles. I scraped a little of the residual oil from his back to massage his firm round cheeks. Most men seem to like their ass worked on in a non-threatening non-sexual way. Q-Dong was no different and he was soon moaning softly as I kneaded his butt cheeks like fine bread dough.

Once I'd relaxed him enough I ran my oiled finger down his crack until I reached his ass hole. I greased it with my fingers and before Q-Dong could resist, I unsheathed the suppository and inserted it between his ass lips, pushing it home with my middle finger. It must have stung because Q-Dong bucked against me. He probably felt betrayed and in pain but I slapped his cheek hard to give him something else to think about. He complained bitterly that I hurt him.

"Okay, pretty boy, it's over. That's a powerful pain killer. If you just lie still." I pulled his briefs back up to cover his anal modesty, "Take a nap, you'll feel like the king of the world when you wake up."

"I doubt it," he mumbled. "No one has ever managed to cure these headaches in the past."

"I bet no one has ever used a magic finger on you before either."

He tried to stifle a laugh. "They wouldn't dare."

"I'm going out to see if I can hunt down your tormentors and warn them off. Once they get a good look at me, I think they'll see reason."

"Hmm, not sure about that. They might think you're hotter than I am what with all those muscles and that python you've got curled up in your pants."

So, he had noticed.

I swatted his butt. "Don't answer the door to anyone unless it's an emergency. Try to get a little sleep. Then you'll feel much better."

After I confirmed with front-of-house security that they'd intercepted the two tormentors, tracing them via their seat numbers as they entered the auditorium, and corralled them in a spare dressing room I marched down the corridor toward our confrontation. Before I entered the room, I drew myself up to my most imposing size, pulled the sleeves of my shirt up to expose my bulging biceps and opened a few buttons to show pecs that would have made a blonde starlet of the 1950s green with envy. You could never be too imposing when dealing with dickheads.

Blake always loved it when I acted tough. He said I was sexier than ever when I tried to act threatening. I just hoped these two bozos would not agree with him. I knocked and one of the security guys opened up. He headed back on duty and I locked the door after him, placing the keys in my pocket.

The two young guys who had caused so much misery to Q-Dong sized me up. In the seconds before they feigned indifference, obviously the 'cool' reaction to my stature, I notice first fear then lust in their eyes. I could work with that. They acted the bad boy routine well but anyone with even limited psychology could see it was mainly cosmetic: from their leather jackets which were more fashion than biker, their leather boots that were so clean they obviously rarely wore them, through to their bad boy shirts which showed off pierced nipples. They had tasteful tats, and their ears, nose, eyebrows, and I thought I noticed a glint on their tongues, were pierced, sometimes multiple.

I introduced myself as Vlad. I glanced at the sheet on the table upon which one of the two men had his feet rested. It was a provocation I was only too happy to take up.

"Which one of you is Bi-ho?"

The guy with his feet on the table grunted. "I'll take that as a yes. Get your feet off the table."

He made no effort to do as I asked. Sarcasm might help. "Please?"

That had no effect either. I walked to where Bi-ho lounged in his plastic chair, my crotch level with his face. He stared at my package so I made it twitch for him. He looked up into my eyes. He removed his feet quick smart, his mate trembling slightly in the plastic chair next to him. I sat my ass on the edge of the desk and placed my big booted feet between their legs, perilously close to their bulges. One quick move and their nuts would be splattered all over their thighs.

I turned to Bi-ho's mate. "You must be Ha-joon?"

He snapped out his answer. "Yes, sir." I do like it when cute guys call me 'sir', especially Blake.

"You've been sending texts to Q-Dong threatening all sorts of sexual humiliation on his body?"

"No way," Bi-ho bluffed. "Why would we do that?"

I shrugged. "Maybe because he's a cute fucker." I already had Q-Dong's cell phone in my hand and rang the number from which the last message was sent. Sure enough, there was a ring tone from Bi-ho's jacket.

"I guess that answers that question." I placed Q-Dong's phone on the desk. "I know you guys run his unofficial gay fan club but that does not give you the right to harass the singer. Right now it's touch and go whether he performs tonight because your text messages have got him so rattled he won't go onstage."

"See I told you," Ha-joon said, turning on his mate. "Now look what we've done."

Bi-ho's bravado evaporated. "We came all this way to hear him sing. It will be so shit if he doesn't. Oh, man." He'd suddenly become a disappointed fan boy.

"Here's what we're gonna do," I said. "You two will text him one more time, telling him how sorry you are for your abusive behavior and promising it will never happen again. That way I might just be able to get him back on stage. If you don't, I will ensure that everyone in the audience knows you two are responsible for Q-Dong's no show. If you're lucky, you might escape unharmed."

Ha-joon already had his cell phone out, his thumbs flying across the keyboards. "No need to do that."

I merely had to look at Bi-ho, not even giving him my death stare, before he joined his mate.

When they completed their humiliating task, they looked at me in expectation. I picked up Q-Dong's phone and read their apologies. Satisfactory.

"Now, that wasn't hard, was it?"

I received reluctant grunts as a response.

"Because you've been such good boys, how about you hang around after the show and, if Q-Dong feels up to it, I'll bring you back stage and introduce you to your hero."

"Really?" Ha-joon almost creamed himself in his seat.

I nodded.

"That would be so cool," Bi-ho said, his bad boy image slipping even further.

I escorted them to the front entrance, showing them where to wait after the concert, and went back to my 'patient.' I felt drained, exhausted. My pep-up pill didn't seem to be working.

I let myself into Q-Dong's dressing room expecting him to be napping still, but he was up and active, practically bouncing off the walls. He raced over to me and flung his arms around my neck. For a moment I thought he was about to kiss me. "You're a miracle man," he gushed. "Headache gone. Feel like I could take on the world. This will be my best performance ever." He was so close I could easily have taken advantage of him but I realized I must have inserted a speed suppository instead of a painkiller up his butt by accident.

No wonder my energy was flagging; I had the painkiller in my ass. At least I wouldn't have a headache tonight.

"I'm thinking of trying something different tonight. How do you think I'd look if I oiled up my body?"

"You'd be hot no matter how you looked."

He gazed at me quizzically. "Hot as in temperature or hot as in…"

"Totally fuckable," I replied honestly.

His lip curled up mischievously. "You'd fuck me?"

"Hell, yeah. But I'm a professional. I don't mix business with pleasure."

"You're gay?"

"Yeah. If that worries you, I can get one of the other security guys to swap."

"That's not necessary. I trust you. Even if you did put your finger up my ass."

"I had to–" I began.

"I know why," he interrupted. To show there were no hard feelings he handed me the baby oil. "Rub me down. I feel mischievous tonight."

"My boyfriend will be so envious when he finds out I oiled you."

"Is he here in Seoul with you?" Q-Dong asked.

"Nah, he's an actor and he's on location with a movie."

"Anyone I would know?" he asked.

I know he was only being polite but the conversation filled in the silences.

"I doubt it. He's most famous for a vampire soap opera he does back home. It's called *Blood Oath*."

I couldn't read the strange look that came over him. "You don't mean your boyfriend is Blake Kendall?"

"You know him?"

"I can't believe he's gay. Is he really your boyfriend?"

I nodded my head proudly. "He wants me to get your autograph because he's a huge fan of yours. Has all your CDs."

The way Q-Dong went on for the next ten minutes, I think we had a mutual admiration society going.

"If you like, after the show, I can ring him and you can talk to him."

Q-Dong was all for that.

"Which reminds me," I added.

I handed him his phone and he read the groveling apologies from his tormentors. He wasn't quite as happy when I informed him they were coming backstage after the concert to meet their idol but, once I assured him I'd be on hand, he relaxed.

The concert had begun and it was piped through the Tannoy into the dressing room. The audience sounded like a riot in progress making it difficult to hear the singers. I guess that didn't matter to most of them, it was their involvement in the mass hysteria that counted.

Q-Dong was caught up in it, jittery, pacing like a caged animal as he admired his glistening physique in the mirror, tweaking his nipples to full erection while his cock writhed from its slumber. He couldn't go out like that, he'd be arrested. He must have realized the same thing as he attempted to push it every which way, including between his legs which had to hurt, all to no avail. "I'll have to wear my jeans," he complained. "I don't know what's wrong with me, I've never been this sexed up before a gig before. After, yes, never before."

I wasn't about to confess to my hand in it. Or should that be finger.

"Channel that nervous energy into your performance and you'll have millions of new fans."

"You think I look good?" he asked with a twinkle in his eye.

"Good enough to eat," I replied.

It was definitely the wrong thing to say.

"Then eat me." He slid down the front of his leather shorts, exposing his beautiful cock that was oozing enough pre-cum that I could smell it from the other side of the room. It took super-human willpower not to drop to my knees and blow this Korean pop god, but I was a professional and I knew it was the speed talking.

"How about you go into the bathroom and jerk off. At the most I'll go find you a female groupie who'll blow you. How's that sound?"

"Disappointing," he said, heading for the bathroom, pouting like a spoilt child. There was much theatrical groaning and a lot of 'Suck it, Vlad' which I assume was to tempt me into the bathroom, but I held out. Finally, a string of curses and a few grunts and it was all over. Q-Dong came back into the dressing room looking much relieved, the bulge in his shorts less prominent.

"Better?" I asked.

"Asshole," he replied, but at least he was smiling.

* * * *

A very nervous PA knocked on the dressing room door about forty minutes later. He'd left it until the last possible moment to ascertain if Q-Dong was going to perform. I could see he had his fingers crossed as I allowed him into the room but his face said it all when he saw Q-Dong seated peacefully at his mirrored table going through the song sheet for the evening. The PA glanced at me in admiration.

"Whatever it is that you did, I'll see that management slips you a bonus."

Before I could tell him no bonus was necessary, he'd approached the temperamental star, asking him to come down to the band's room for last minute briefing. He wasn't nearly as pleased when Q-Dong stood to reveal his near naked body glistening with oil, highlighting his muscles, his package, and his ass. I sensed there could be trouble brewing but the PA had no chance of winning any argument with Q-Dong that night.

It was a relief when I was left to my own company and I took those few minutes to disappear into the bathroom with my fanny pack. The door firmly locked, I found another suppository that would give me the extra strength I needed to get through the night. It was the twin of the one that had been wedged up Q-Dong's butt by mistake. I would have to label them more carefully in future.

By the time I felt the effects and my blood started pumping, Q-Dong was on stage to the most amazing reception. I went to watch on the monitor in the Green Room. It was quite a show and if it hadn't been for the hysteria and the fact any police intervention might have been met with a full-scale riot, Q-Dong came perilously close to being arrested. Even some members of the band seemed surprised at the singer's provocative antics as he threw himself about the stage with super-human energy, thrusting his crotch and his ass at the audience, playing with his own nipples, licking his lips in the most lascivious manner. Yep, I was hard. I only hoped the promoters would release a DVD of the show so I could get a copy for Blake. It would be a better than my feeble attempts to describe the concert.

I was backstage as NQB8 did their third and final encore. The audience didn't want to let them go but there was transport to catch, parties to attend, groupies to take care of. I ensured that Q-Dong wasn't crushed in the melee in the corridors as every wanna-be journalist and Z-List celebrity begged for a moment to bathe in Q-Dong's glory. I managed to clear a path and get him to his dressing room in one piece, pushing the door closed on a bevy of expectant faces.

Q-Dong bounced on the balls of his feet. He was still high from the speed and his performance. He wouldn't come down for hours.

"What do you want?" I asked.

"I can't relax just yet, let them in. They all want their piece of me. Tonight they can have it. I was never better, you know. That was the most amazing concert."

I agreed. "You were. I watched in the Green Room. You were…amazing."

Q-Dong kissed me briefly on the cheek by standing on tip toes. "Thanks to you."

"Will you be okay? I have to get your cell phone stalkers."

"Yeah. I know how to handle myself."

Hurrying through the building which seemed to be a more frenetic hive of activity now the concert was over than it was during the preparation, I found Bi-ho and Ha-joon bubbling with excitement near the stage door.

"Oh my God," Ha-joon shrieked. "Did you see him? He was sooo good. I can't believe we're going to meet him."

Bi-ho was obviously as blown away but attempted a nonchalance that was obviously an act, until I ushered them through the door. "You really are taking us to meet him? Oh fuck."

The two stalkers were so in awe of their surroundings I thought they'd both come on the spot. They were like wide-eyed teenagers as they passed dressing room after dressing room of famous boy bands clustered with admirers. There were constant unfinished sentences of "That's…" and "That can't be…" They weren't just talking about the singers but also the VIP guests that crowded the venue.

By the time we pushed our way into Q-Dong's dressing room, they seemed so overwhelmed I thought they'd cry. Q-Dong acknowledged them with a curt nod of the head as he played to the crowd. It was becoming a crush when I closed it down. Although Q-Dong blamed security when the visitors grizzled about 'high-handedness' and 'typical European bullying', Q-Dong smiled his appreciation at my action. As soon as the door closed, Q-Dong turned his attention to his stalkers.

Now that they could see him in his near nakedness, I noticed movement in their groins. Q-Dong noticed as well. "See something you like?"

Suddenly Bi-ho and Ha-joon were tongue tied.

Q-Dong turned to me. "Vlad, would you mind getting me some sparkling mineral water from the Green Room?"

I knew he had full bottles in the bar fridge in the dressing room so he wanted time alone with these two. I knew he could handle himself and the poor stalkers were so over-awed they'd be no trouble at all.

"If there's any trouble you know how to contact me," I lied.

Q-Dong watched them squirm. "And Vlad. Take your time."

I guessed Q-Dong was about to chew them both a new asshole for the stress they'd put him through.

I'd been in the Green Room, oh, about ten to fifteen minutes with a well-deserved cold beer when the fraught PA come bustling up to me. "Come quickly. Q-Dong's dressing room is locked and there are terrible sounds of a fight inside. I'm worried."

I shot off my stool and down the winding maze of corridors before the PA had finished his request. I'd never forgive myself if anything happened. Yes, there were sounds of some sort of ruckus from the room, including groans of what could be intense pain. I slid the key into the lock and burst into the room. Q-dong looked up. "Come in and close the door. Join the party."

Turning to intercept the PA who tried to peer around my body, I said, "Everything is in order. Q-Dong is just tearing strips off the two young men who sent him those obscene texts. He's fine."

The PA was about to say something when I closed the door very politely in his face.

"Thanks," Q-Dong said. At least I think that's what he said because it was muffled by the long thin cock that had disappeared into his mouth. It belonged to Ha-joon.

The two stalkers looked a little concerned at my entrance but as Q-Dong was not struggling, I guessed that the behavior was consensual. That was confirmed when he spat out Ha-joon's cock and invited me to take his place. Ha-Joon must have been close to orgasm because he cursed loudly and his cock shot all over the kneeling singer's face, coating it with a huge dump of spooge. God, that was so hot. Q-Dong licked cum from his mouth and chin where his tongue could reach. I strode over to wipe the spunk from around his eyes.

Bi-ho didn't hesitate for a moment as he plowed his cock up the asshole in which I'd inserted a suppository of almost pure speed earlier. "You suddenly decided to explore your gay side or did these guys talk you into it?"

Ha-joon stumbled over his words in an attempt to make excuses. "He spread his legs and told us to fuck him. Honest."

"His ass is so fuckin' tight I think he's squeezed my cock half to death," Bi-ho puffed as he continued to slide his nice-sized cock in and out of the singer's guts.

Okay, so I had an erection. I wouldn't be human if I hadn't been turned on. Didn't mean I was going to join in. My career would be over if word got around, but I wasn't gonna stop the action either.

"Come on, Vlad. Let me taste you?" Q-Dong begged.

Fuck! You know just how difficult it is to say no when one of the hottest pop stars in the universe is begging for your cock. It was hell on earth.

"Can't. Hold. On. Much. Longer," Bi-ho panted. I watched his ass cheeks clench and his body shudder as he emptied his balls right up Q-Dong's chute.

Watching the scene unfold put me in serious danger if I didn't release my cock soon. I needn't have concerned myself because I felt a pair of hands at work on my belt and my zipper. Because I knew it wasn't Q-Dong I closed my eyes as my trousers and briefs were pulled down to let the air cool my overheated nuts.

Ha-joon wasted no time in licking the pre-cum oozing from my slit, his tongue stud rubbing below the head of my cock. He opened his mouth wide to accommodate my thick sausage and almost choked.

"Take it easy, mate," I said stroking his hair. "It's not a competition."

"Get away from his cock," Q-Dong demanded. "It's mine."

"Bossy little bitch, aren't you?" I replied. "Get over here."

Q-Dong scrambled to his feet, his well-fucked hole squelching as he approached. I held his handsome cum-spattered face as I looked into his eyes. "That's how you should be all the time. Covered in man spunk. It makes you even more beautiful."

"If it's yours, I'll wear it until it dries then beg you for more."

Bi-ho hung back uncertainly. I motioned for him to join his mate worshipping my cock. Two tongues are sometimes better than one when the one is struggling to get it all down his throat.

I held Q-Dong tightly to my side, turning my head sideways to lick the spunk off his face. He tried to capture my darting tongue with his mouth but until I'd siphoned up all the slime, I was too quick for him. Then I pushed my oozing tongue inside so he could taste Ha-joon's juice. Q-Dong was an extraordinary kisser. Even Blake wasn't this good and he was the best I'd ever met.

My neck was cramping from the unnatural position so I picked Q-Dong up in my arms, cradling him against my chest so I could suction his tongue with what I hoped was half the skill that he managed on mine.

The two stalkers were licking my shaft and taking turns attempting to deep throat me, to varying degrees of success. I let them practice for a while but I was too far gone now to care if I lost my job or not. I had to get inside Q-Dong. Fuck the consequences.

I gently pushed aside the two guys attacking my cock with their mouths in order to carry Q-Dong to the divan. I laid him on his back. He knew what I was after and immediately spread his legs, holding them aloft so his leaking ass winked his desire. I took my time stripping off my clothes as I was perilously close to losing my load. Once totally naked, my cock now seen in proportion to my body, fleeting concern clouded Q-Dong's face. I was at least twice the size of Bi-ho so Q-Dong must have realized I was gonna hurt. Bad. I didn't know if I would be able to stop once I was inside him, even if he begged.

Stroking my cock with a palm of baby oil to get my monster well lubricated, I used the other hand to oil his hole and slip a finger inside him to explore for his prostate. I knew I'd found it when I ran my finger over a small bump and Q-Dong's cock bucked.

The two stalkers stood watching, offering comments that were in danger of turning me off my allotted task.

"Fuck me!" the man below me screamed. "Get your cock inside me now!"

He was not to be disobeyed. He could have my nuts for garters, my job, my whole career, if I didn't obey him. That was my excuse. I tucked thoughts of my boyfriend back home to one side and concentrated on the hot man beneath me, his legs spread apart revealing his puckered purple hole that dribbled lubrication and the remnants of the earlier fuck. I positioned the throbbing head of my prick at his entrance; it looked much too small to take my cock.

"Don't do it, dude." Bi-ho warned. "You'll tear him apart with that monster."

"Come on," Ha-joon said, cringing as I pushed ever-so-gently against my prey's sphincter. "He'll rip you apart."

"Shut the fuck up," the subject of all this pseudo concern screamed. Turning to me, he demanded, "Give it to me hard."

I slammed my meat into the tightest, warmest asshole I'd ever fucked. I groaned as his ass muscles clenched around my cock, his breath hissing between his teeth as the pain stabbed home, his mates cringing as his hole stretched to the limit to accommodate my girth.

He'd placed his hands on my thighs to signal he needed time to adjust to the fullness in his butt. I watched as he tentatively withdrew one hand, then the other. He looked into my eyes dreamily as I began to saw my cock gently in and out of his ass. I would get much rougher later.

He burbled his satisfaction, then asked, "Why don't you ring your vampire boyfriend?"

I snapped my fingers, indicating to one of the others to get my phone from my trousers. They swung into action and soon I was focusing my cell phone camera on the man who was stuck on the end of my prick. I withdrew so only the head was inside and then I snapped the pic – as much for me as for Blake. I wasn't sure what his reaction would be once I'd sent it to him.

"He won't mind?" Q-Dong asked as I pumped back inside him.

"I'll soon find out."

I had counted twenty in my head when my ring tone echoed around the room. I put the cell phone on speaker and Blake's voice boomed, "Is that who I think it is wriggling like a cock lollipop on the end of your dick?"

I laughed. "Who does it look like?"

"Please tell me it's Q-Dong. Please tell me he loves having his ass fucked and that you're doing him."

"Why don't you ask him yourself?"

"You put me on speaker phone? You bastard!"

Q-Dong laughed. "Yes, it's me. Are you really Blake Kendall? You're my favorite actor."

"You're my favorite singer."

"How soon can you get here so I can get your cock in my ass as well?"

"I'm on location. Sorry."

"Pity."

This fan club meeting was threatening the sexual tension and I had to bring an end to it. I slammed my cock as hard as I could into Q-Dong who let out a peep of surprise and a groan of pain/pleasure.

"Oh my God," Blake said. I heard him lower the zip on his pants.

"Are you playing with your cock, Blake?" I asked.

"What do you reckon, mate? Shoot me some footage so I can see what's going on while I jerk off."

I appealed to Q-Dong who nodded his agreement. I instructed the guys to get Q-dong's phone and film me for a few minutes pounding his tight asshole, getting a close-up of his ass lips stretching around my weapon as it threatened to split him in two. Q-dong was very vocal in his appreciation of my prowess and Blake could hear every second of it.

"You got your private cell phone with you?" I enquired.

"Yeah, why?"

"I'll send the footage so you can see us while you listen."

I heard Blake scrambling to get his spare, instructing Bi-ho on the number to send the footage to.

While all this was going on, I felt fingers exploring my butt hole. Ha-joon was getting adventurous.

"Go for it, mate," I called over my shoulder.

I felt the baby oil being squirted on my crack, then being massaged into my hole before a cock poked at my entrance. I stopped balling Q-Dong to allow Ha-joon to penetrate me. I loved cock in my ass almost as much as I loved my cock in someone else's ass. Ha-joon sank in easily, muttering a few fucks as I tightened my sphincter around him.

Bi-ho sent off the short video and soon had his cock buried down Q-Dong's throat. Selfishly, I regretted not being able to see my cute singer's face as I brought him off, but if I held off my orgasm long enough, Bi-ho would dump his load and leave my boy's face for me to lavish with kisses.

"Fuckin' hell, dude, that footage is so fuckin' hot. I'm telling you, if I wasn't on location, I'd be on the next plane to Seoul just so I could get my cock buried in that tight hole. Or fuck his cute face. Or…"

Blake kept up his tirade of what he wanted to do to Q-Dong and I imagined the two of us doing the Korean pop star together. I was peaking but I slowed my pace to give Bi-ho his opportunity and because I loved the feel of Ha-joon's cock embedded in my ass. How much greater if it had been Q-Dong's. Maybe there'd be an opportunity for a repeat.

Bi-ho gritted his teeth and grunted. I saw Q-Dong's throat muscles at work. He must have been swallowing the spunk that was flooding his mouth. When Bi-ho withdrew, Q-Dong licked his lips all the while staring into my eyes. I felt Ha-joon shove harder and his juice squirted inside me. He slumped against my back for a few moments before pulling out. That left me free to fuck Q-Dong as hard as he was begging, as hard as Blake was telling me to do it.

I pulled back, my ass rising in the air, and let gravity take over, my body slamming Q-Dong into the divan as my cock found places it hadn't penetrated before. I did that a few times until I thought Q-Dong would expire from either the pain or the pure pleasure so I went back to varying my thrusts.

Ha-joon and Bi-ho must have dressed and let themselves out as I buggered Q-Dong because they weren't in the room when I bellowed that I was about to blow my prodigious load. I heard Blake increase his strokes over the phone as I took aim with my cock at that little nub inside Q-Dong's ass and plunged across it time after time until I heard him moan, his own cock flooding his belly with spunk. His sphincter clenched way too tight for me to hold back and I swamped his anal cavity with my cum.

Q-Dong and I were both showered and dressed when the PA tapped tentatively at the dressing room door. I let him in. He was there to take Q-Dong to a party to which I knew I would not be welcome. He looked saddened that he couldn't take me. It wouldn't have mattered because I had things to wrap up at the stadium.

"It's been a real pleasure, Q-Dong," I said. "I'll miss you."

He smiled broadly, his eyes sparkling. "Not for long." He turned to his PA. "When is it we tour Australia?"

"We're still in negotiations," the PA replied. "It will likely be some time in October."

"And we will need security?" Q-Dong asked.

"Definitely."

"Will you be available, Vlad?" he asked.

"I will make myself available," I replied.

"And Blake will be available, too?"

"I'm sure he will be if he knows you're coming."

"Oh, we'll all be coming," Q-Dong smiled. "Over and over and over again."

"Blake and I will be looking forward to it."

I watched as Q-Dong walked down the corridor to the stage door. Without turning, he wiggled his beautiful butt as he turned the corner. I was looking forward to making its re-acquaintance.

FROM TOP TO BOTTOM

It was the adult son of the aged couple next door who told me about it. I was just pulling my drooling dick out of his ass after I'd plugged him, not for the first time, now that I'd returned to the family nest after four years at university.

While I was away, the Munroes had moved in after the demise of old Mr. Stone who must have been in his nineties – he'd lived in the house all his life. The Munroes had a son in his late thirties who my mum whispered was a 'confirmed bachelor.' In our small city that meant only one thing. Don't bend over in the back yard.

However, young Ferdie Munroe, was a looker. Had a body on him like a professional wrestler, one of those beefcake dudes with the fake names and the fake personalities. I know because I was a fan. So, it turned out, was Ferdie who used to invite me over to watch the matches on the cable channel on his widescreen TV. There's a rumor that the bigger the screen, the smaller the cock, but in Ferdie's case, it simply wasn't true.

He had a mammoth prick when it was hard, which seemed to be just about all the time. So after I'd finished plugging his warm tight butthole he thought it was only fair that I bend over and take his nine-inches of stud meat.

"I don't bottom," I said proudly. "No one gets near my ass, especially not with something that looks like it belongs on a horse."

I suddenly realized that could have come across as offensive but Ferdie looked mighty proud after my description.

"So you think I'm horse hung, eh?"

"I'd bet money on it. Put you up beside the best stallion in the country and I guarantee you'd come up the winner." It didn't hurt to lay on the flattery.

In the end it didn't help because he immediately changed the subject back to my ass.

"So you never been fucked, eh?"

"Nope."

"So how do you know you won't like it?"

"I've had a doctor or two finger my butthole and another poke some sort of surgical instrument where the sun don't shine, and let me tell you their fingers and the implement put together weren't as big as that monster you've got between your legs. And those doctors hurt like the devil."

"So what am I supposed to do? You got your rocks off, now I'm all hot and bothered."

"I'll give you a hand job. Don't mind that," I said giving his dick a friendly wank.

"I can do that myself," he sulked. "What about a blow job?"

"Not keen on giving them," I admitted. "I don't think I could fit that in my mouth."

"How about you try?" Ferdie looked like he was not about to take 'no' for an answer.

Okay, I got myself into this predicament. Ferdie had read all the signals correctly when I'd got hard as hell in my shorts while we were watching The Boston Mangler wrestle this gorgeous dark haired mother called Squadron, supposedly because he had the power of ten men. Who cared, the guy was heaven on a stick? Ferdie and I both had our tongue hanging out panting over The Squad as he pummeled Boston into the mat. I don't know what Ferdie was fantasizing but I had visions of Squad's hot naked body, pretty face down, as my cock pounded his hard bubble butt.

Ferdie reached across and squeezed my obvious hard-on. I did the same to him. A few minutes later I was buried in his ass rather than Squad's and it made a very nice substitute indeed. My neighbor's boy was hot as buggery and I was looking forward to taking further advantage of his hospitality and his open ass every chance I could get.

Until he asked for reciprocal visitation rights.

This was our third time watching the wrestling together. The first two had been sounding each other out. Within ten minutes I'd discovered my mother's description of Ferdie was apt, while he took a little while longer to suss me out. Gave me the chance to play mind games which I love doing.

The first time we had sex he'd been content with my cock up his ass, bringing himself off while I was fucking him. A few visits later, he pushed me down to my knees and prodded an inch or two into my inexperienced mouth. I intended to keep it that way although he seemed to be equally determined to give me the experience he thought I needed against my will. In the end I had my lips wrapped around a couple of inches of his cock while holding it from further penetration with my fist. He was equally determined to push it all the way into my throat. There was never a proper conclusion to our stalemate because the friction against his shaft and the small amount of knob licking I was performing obviously did the trick and he shot onto my tongue.

No way was I gonna swallow all that spooge, so I politely spat it into a tissue.

Ferdie watched aghast as I scrunched up his precious body fluid and threw it in the bin. Turning to me, he said, "Not very experienced are you?"

I was smug "No one's complained yet."

"Until now," he said knocking my complacency out of the ball park.

"Well, if you don't like what I do, I don't have to come over and watch the wrestling with you, but I thought the way you screamed like a stuck pig as I fucked you, that you were enjoying yourself."

When you're young and gorgeous, like I am, then you can dictate your terms. I'm twenty-one, a real twink with blond hair, hot, firm body, a bubble butt which you can admire, sniff or lick, but otherwise don't touch. A tongue is permissible, a finger is not. And a cock will get you a black eye. My cock is a nice plump eight inches and I've never had a complaint. Until now. I might add I'm as good looking as any Hollywood star you care to name. Only downside to my utter gorgeiosity, my word, is that I tend more toward the pretty than the rugged so guys think they're gonna get into my ass, whereas if I looked like a wharfie they'd expect my cock. Too bad, there's nothing I can do about it.

You don't like it, go harass some other poor fucker who hasn't got half the appeal I've got. I don't need the hassle. I've got admirers to spare. Especially back in this small pond. No one's seen me in four years. I went away an ugly duckling and I've come back a fuckin' swan. In fact, I'm too good for most of the miserable bastards who eke out some sort of sexual existence in this berg.

I should be in New York or San Francisco, London or Amsterdam, Berlin or Rome showing those fuckers what real beauty is all about. People stare open mouthed when I walk by. They can't believe how good looking I am, or what a hot body I have. They all want a piece of me. Plus I dance like a fuckin' angel, I fuck like the devil himself and I got the personality that makes God envious.

Yeah, you may think I come across as arrogant or conceited, but I'm just tellin' it like it is, baby. You want me, it's on my terms. And you better be one hot fucker yourself with an asshole that likes insatiable cock. That's what I am, fuckin' insatiable. Never met anyone yet that can tame my prick. Not idle boasting either. Pop a Viagra and I can perform for days. Couple of big producers wanted to make me a star in pornos. Nope, I'm gonna go legit. Modeling or Hollywood. That gives you some idea of just how hot I am. Think of sizzling, then quadruple it.

Got it now?

Seems Ferdie never got it right. Sure, he wanted my cock in his shit-hole on a regular basis and I was happy to oblige. Fuck, why not? He's right next door. The only thing more convenient would be if assholes were delivered. But he kept moaning about me giving up my hole to him. I learned to take his cock most of the way down my throat just to get him to keep his trap shut with the woe and the misery.

I could have easily taken the whole fuckin' dick, knob and all down my gullet but I like to preserve a little mystery. Made it easier to take him blasting a load inside my mouth. If the cock's in your throat it bypasses your taste buds and your swallow muscles, just heads straight down to your stomach acid without you having to do anything. Those crazy intestines take care of everything.

So I was surprised, pleasantly, when Ferdie didn't bang on about his fuckin' 'needs' on that particular day. What? He thinks I don't have needs of my own? But he did mention The Party. I knew it was a big deal. I heard the capitals in the way he said it. I was intrigued.

Even in a city the size of the one where I found myself stranded until I could make the bucks to head to the sin capitals overseas, I was running out of partners my equal. It was one of the reasons I kept returning to Ferdie, apart from the convenience. He was hot, and when he wasn't sulking, he was a great lay.

"I'll nail that ass of yours one day," he'd joke after every session. It was getting very tedious. Time for new pastures. There had to be some good looking men in the town, apart from Ferdie.

I'd got a bit desperate at times and let a couple of guys not quite up to my usual standards sample the goods. A couple more who looked promising wanted to breach the security area around my ass and I had to tell them, sometimes in less than friendly terms, no way!

So when Ferdie mentioned The Party he had me and my cock's undivided attention.

"Biggest party on the gay map in this city," he said proudly.

"Anyone of importance is there, people come from all over and they have the best backroom for all-out fucking like you've never seen before. Goes on all weekend."

My cock twitched its approval.

"How do I get a ticket?"

"Just so happens I have a spare," Ferdie gloated.

I knew where this was going.

"I can pay for my own." I just couldn't be fucked going through the hassle of begging Ferdie if he was going to barter the ticket for my ass.

"No strings attached," Ferdie said. "It's yours for the asking."

"Well, I'm asking, mate."

It was a couple of weeks away yet so I knew Ferdie may not be expecting my ass in return but he was definitely expecting to be fucked on a regular basis. That was easily fixed and his mouth and his ass got a periodic servicing. I had to beware, it was getting too damn comfortable just ducking next door whenever the urge hit. Fortunately, Ferdie had the granny flat attached to his parents' house so we were never interrupted and my parents thought it was good I'd made a friend even if he was a 'confirmed bachelor."

I overheard my mum and dad discussing it one night.

"Shane knows how to take care of himself if that fag tried anything."

"I don't think they care for that word, dear," mum admonished.

"Whatever word it goes by, I know Shane won't be bested."

Fuckin' right, dad.

I suppose I could have gone the route so many good looking dudes have gone before to make a start. I could have sold my cock by the inch but the idea of some old cunt hanging off my dick or massaging my balls with his gummy mouth revolted me. I'd have to find some other lucrative possibility. I'd asked Ferdie if he knew some way to make a small fortune quick smart. He had a few ideas, like the preceding one but they all involved me doing things that would have curdled fuckin' milk.

He warned me to play it cool at the party, that I was getting quite a reputation around town.

"A reputation's a good thing to have," I preened.

"Not when it's a bad one like you've got. Quite a few guys would like to see you taken down a peg or two. They'd pay good money for that."

Try as I might I could think of no way to turn that to my advantage.

Life went on as before in the lead up to the party. My parents kept bugging me about my future. God, give it a fuckin' rest. Look at me, I'm unbelievably hot. If I can just find a way out of Deadwood Gulch I'd be on top of the world.

Problem was I had no one to confide in, so I guess that's how I started telling Ferdie things that I would've been better off keeping mum about. Still, I could see no harm in telling him my fantasies. Except he kept trying to crush them. Like when he said, "The world is full of gorgeous men, Shane. What have you got that the others haven't?"

"D'uh, hello," I said. "Look at me."

"I'm looking," he said. "I see a hot guy with a good body, what else you got to offer?"

I unzipped because I knew that was what he was after. He was down on his knees faster than a slutty nun at confession. He had my balls purring in no time and I was dumping my first load within ten minutes as Ferdie worked his oral magic on my wang.

As he wiped his mouth, he looked up into my eyes and kept the conversation going. "Yeah, great cock but unless you're going into porn what else you got going for you?"

"That's the trouble with this country, Ferdie. It thinks small. Overseas, beauty is its own reward."

"Right," he said and I thought I detected the smallest trace of sarcasm. "So you think in New York your beauty will…what?"

"It'll open the most amazing fuckin' doors. All you gotta do there is stand on a street corner and the crowds who see me will weep because I'm so hot and they can't touch. Some dude will pull up in a limo, open the door and I'll be on my way."

"To where, mate?"

"To wherever gods like me go to make their fame and fortune."

"Where exactly is that, mate?"

God, the prick was irritating. Always wanting the details. They'd work themselves out once I got to where the god-like people walked the earth. Not here in Pricksville. I really would have to reappraise my friendship with Ferdie. Once the party was over. The cunt was so negative, always trying to bring me down. Jealous as fuck, I'd say. His own miserable existence working in a gas station at night while he studied God knows what to better himself.

Stupid prick, who needs education? I never did.

Truth is, I never went to university. I thought the cunts would have realized that. But the bastards never asked what courses I took. Just accepted my parents' word. No one wondered why I never came home for a visit in those four years. Hah! I was in The Resort. Hot showers, your own room, three meals a day, library, television, all the mod cons. In fact that's what the resort was for: mod cons.

Attempted robbery. Six years with non-parole period of four. I kept my nose clean but not my knob. Sure a few guys tried it on but they soon learned I may be cute but I'm fuckin' lethal. I guess my parents thought university sounded classier than prison, so we called it The Resort on the very few occasions it was ever mentioned, usually in anger, at home.

It was just like my fuckin' old man to be pissed off because I got caught for 'attempted' robbery. "You couldn't even pull that one off right. Christ, son. I'd be proud of you if you'd pulled it off then got caught, but you didn't even get away with it."

Parents can be such a downer sometimes.

As the big weekend approached I asked Ferdie, "What's the dress code for this party?"

"Anything sexy. You can strip naked once you're in the door."

"Gotcha. Wear something ordinary to get in the door, then strip down to the barest necessities once inside. And you reckon there'll be loads of hot men there?"

"You bet."

It would be good to stick my blue-pilled prick into some new anal glove. Ferdie was getting on my wick, always smiling at me as if something was going on in that brain of his.

I told mum not to expect me home all weekend because I was heading out of town for a party. She knew better than to warn me to be careful so she settled for "Enjoy yourself."

"Oh, I will," I said.

Dad just muttered something about getting a job but I pretended not to hear the prick.

I met Ferdie at the end of the street away from my mum's prying eyes: I knew she'd be at the window watching me. I didn't want her to think I was *that* friendly with the neighborhood fag. He had the tickets, the booze to get us nicely lubricated before we got there, and enough recreationals to drop a horse although he assured me we'd be able to buy plenty on site.

I had to stay close to Ferdie because my cash reserves were running low. Mum had taken to hiding her purse so that avenue had dried up. Dad's wallet was as elusive as the Bermuda Triangle so I was down to my last few bucks. If there were mind altering substances to purchase, or booze for that matter, I'd need a friend. Ferdie was predictable, he'd be so stoned within an hour of arriving it'd be easy enough to lift his wallet and credit cards.

We seemed to drive for ages but Ferdie assured me it was off the beaten track so revelers wouldn't be disturbed.

"It's an old whaling station on the coast that the organizer bought and converted into a warehouse for dance parties. Has all the old machinery, and he's installed slings and racks, everything you could need for a weekend of excess."

I was about to ask about the music when I heard the thump of bass off in the distance.

Party Time.

I'd show these fuckers how to have a good time.

It didn't take long for me to discover I'd been seriously misled. Sure, it was an old whaling station, and it was decked out inside for a whale of a party, but most of what else I'd been told was so much cunting hot air.

According to my calculations, there were about a hundred guys dancing their tits off. None of them held a candle to me. Not even a fuckin' flashlight. I expressed my disappointment to Ferdie.

"It's only early yet," he said. "Guys will turn up all weekend. Most will arrive on Saturday."

"They better be hot," I snarled.

Ferdie got me a drink and the burn of liquor on my throat and stomach calmed me a little, mellowed me out. By the time I was on my third, the crowd seemed to have swelled and I chided myself that I may have been a little hasty in my judgment of their looks and their bodies. Some of them were definitely looking attractive to me now.

Don't get the idea that being gobsmacking gorgeous like I am is all roses. It has its downside. Like the putrid old cunts who buzzed around me like mosquitoes around a bright light. Or is that moths? Anyway, these bloodsuckers were as annoying as that high pitched whine mozzies give out. Problem was I couldn't smack them to death between my hands. Much as I really wanted to.

Some of them even had the nerve to suggest they were saving themselves for my ass later that weekend.

In your dreams.

Obviously wealthier men said they would pay good money to have me alone in a back room for half an hour, while others said they and their mates would pay to watch me strip for their amusement.

I told them all in no uncertain terms what they could do with their offers.

No one seemed offended no matter how rude or obscene I got. They just laughed as if I was some sort of joke.

I tracked down Ferdie who was talking to one of the most offensive guys and tried to yank him away.

"Come on, Shane, I want you to meet our host. Shane, this is Maurice, he's the man responsible for all this glitter and gaiety."

"Oh, I've met Shane before but he turned down my advances. In a none-too-subtle manner, I might add. But I'm a forgiving man. Why don't I give you a tour of the premises? Show you to the VIP Room which may be more to your liking."

"That sounds more like it," I said.

"Nothing is too good for our Shane," he said.

Ferdie and Maurice preceded me up the stairs to what appeared to be a glassed-in enclosure overlooking the party below, but they couldn't see inside. I guessed it was that glass the cops use for interrogations. They can look in but you can't see out. Nifty idea.

Maurice ushered me inside. The place was as dark as an asshole although once I got used to it I could make out a bar at one end with…fuck…a naked guy stirring the drinks with his cock. It put Ferdie to shame by about an inch. It made my eyes water just thinking about it. Other guys were lazing about the leather lounges and divans in various stages of sniffing, snorting and swallowing. A waiter, dressed only in a leather cock ring, carried a tray of multi-colored pills and phials around the room. I didn't notice anyone paying.

The host must have read my mind. "Everything up here is gratis to my guests," he said. "Please feel free in indulge in any way you see fit. You can watch the action downstairs through the mirrored glass or you can help yourself to any of the staff. They are trained to be obedient."

Just then I spied a cute twink with the best ass in the place, even better than Ferdie's.

"Where do you take them?" I asked.

"Anywhere," Maurice smiled.

"Right here?"

"You're not shy, are you?"

"Fuck no!"

I snapped my fingers and the young guy came over immediately. I took the tray from him, handing it to Maurice who looked somewhat non-plussed at being treated like an employee.

"Down, boy!" I commanded the twink who sank to his knees obediently. You gotta love someone who is so attuned to your needs.

I unzipped and hauled out my cock. A few of the other partygoers in the VIP room came over to watch. Hell, nothing like a good crowd.

"Open."

I pushed my already stiff prick into the twink's mouth and kept right on going. He was good, really well trained and took it all the way without a murmur.

"Good boy," Maurice purred. "We pride ourselves on having the best trained staff in the country."

"Enough with the blah blah blah," I snapped.

This guy was an expert. I wondered whether he was drugged although he was as eager to suck me dry as I was to dump a fresh load in his stomach. He used his tongue like my cock was a musical instrument. He played my balls, licking and sucking them until they shone with his spit, my cock slimy with his gag juices even though I'd not heard a whimper from him. You know how buzzy it is to look down and watch your cock and balls thrust out of the fly of your trousers being devoured by some cute twink fuck slave.

If I didn't pace myself I'd fill his mouth before I had a chance at his ass.

"Kneel, fucker!"

As reluctant as I was to have him take his leech-like mouth off my cock, as reluctant as he seemed to be to relinquish it, I wanted his ass bad. I fingered his puckered little hole to discover it was already lubricated. Didn't feel like some other cunt's spooge so I guessed the staff was greased up in anticipation.

I shoved my cock in to a slight 'oomph' from the twink. His anal passage was hot as burning coal as it wrapped around my prick.

"Milk me with your boy cunt, you filthy little slut," I spat at him, slapping his ass as he lowered his head to the floor to give me better access to his ass.

"Fuckin' tight ass I'm gonna flood with my spunk, till your stomach explodes with my slime. Want to see you suck my balls dry. Shoot all over you face until you drown in spunk."

Woo, I was flying. Never felt like this before. It was like my little twink partner was just a pretty hole for my cock. I slammed him, I rammed him, I slapped him, and I bit him. Fuck, this was incredible. I heard people talking about us. Me. How good I was. That they wished they were on the end of my gigantic prick. I could feel it expanding inside his ass, ready to split him open.

"Take my spunk you little slut whore."

He turned his face up to me with the most angelic smile I had ever seen. A smile I wanted to fuck into oblivion.

I screamed as my cock snot shot into his ass and he clenched his sphincter around me to drain every last drop of my man juice.

I fell sweaty and exhausted against his back until I felt hands dragging me to my feet and helping me to one of the leather divans.

"Incredible, Shane. I could always stand a new waiter if you're ever in the market to work here," Maurice said.

"Nah," I replied. "I have bigger dreams than some shitty club on the outskirts of this Shitholeville."

"Always the gracious one," Ferdie mumbled.

"It's good to dream big," Maurice said, patting my shoulder in a manner I found much too familiar but I was too exhausted to do anything about it.

He snapped his fingers and a waiter appeared. "A nice cocktail for Shane, I think. Something to get his strength back after that vigorous exercise with young Darren."

The waiter disappeared to return a short while later with a multi-colored concoction. I had no idea what it was but it was smooth and cool as it went down, heading straight to my cock once it hit my stomach. My balls were on fire; my cock felt like it could conquer the world.

The next few hours, I think they were hours, were a blur of asses and mouths that I plugged, spewing my cream into the anonymous holes. I don't even remember what the guys looked like or even if they were waiters but they had to be cute otherwise I wouldn't have touched them. Right? Although in one sickening moment of clarity I looked down to see this fat old slug of a guy who I'd almost belted in the mouth when he'd propositioned me earlier, sucking my manhood. I knew it was the drugs. I knew it couldn't be him. They wouldn't let someone like that in the VIP Room. Would they?

I must have passed out because I woke up to find I was on a divan in a corner, covered with a blanket.

Shit! What had they done to me while I was out? Gingerly, I felt for my ass but it was dry and tight. They hadn't tried anything.

I staggered to my feet, my cock as sore as if I'd stuck it in a pencil sharpener. I snickered. As if they ever made pencil sharpeners that huge.

A few people where watching the activity below but most seemed to be sleeping off the drugs, the booze, the sexual excess. I had no idea what time it was because there were no windows to the outside world. Ferdie warned me that once inside you stayed until you had enough. Once you left, for whatever reason, there was no re-admittance.

The smell of hot food wafted across the room making my stomach rumble like thunder on a hot summer's day. I staggered toward the pleasing scent of bacon, eggs and…who the fuck cared? Food is food. I pushed open a door to discover a canteen, but a high-class one. There were all types of food piled high in the bains-marie, reminding me a little of the meals at The Resort, although prison never had choices like this. There was smoked salmon, thin as tissue ham, the tastiest bacon, eggs scrambled like clouds, sausages cooked to perfection. My mouth watered.

Grabbing a plate I helped myself to the goodies, piling my plate high until one of the servers reminded me gently that I could come back as many times as I liked. Looking around, I spied Ferdie seated with Maurice and a number of fat bastards who looked like it would have done them good to skip breakfast. In fact skip all meals for a fuckin' week.

I went over and planted myself beside them. They looked at me, so I felt I had to say something.

"Great party, Morrie."

I saw the ice crystals form on his brow.

"Maurice."

What the fuck?

"Yeah," I said as if that was an answer to everything.

"Are you enjoying yourself, Shane?"

"Fuck yeah," I said with such enthusiasm I spat Salmon over the table. "Me knob's rubbed raw from all the fucking and sucking."

"Oh, I do hope you'll have the strength to keep up today. If you need any…uh…help, there's a doctor on the premises who can cater to any need. He has a few items in his little purse that can make one insatiable."

"Fuck, I don't need any stimulants to make me insatiable," I lied. "I'm just naturally horny. I guess you could say my cock is organic like that."

No one else at the table laughed. Humorless fuckers.

The others around the table got up a few minutes later leaving their food half eaten, wasteful cunts. Only Ferdie remained.

"You having a good time?" he asked.

"If I believe my cock, yeah. I just wish I could remember it."

"I saw you a few times. You sure draw a crowd when you're down and dirty. Those poor waiters don't know what hit them. They'll need a week to recover."

"I thought that…" I was about to tell Ferdie about my imagining the fat slug on the end of my prick but I knew it was an hallucination.

"What?"

"Oh, nothing. I gotta stay sober for the next round so I remember."

"Maybe security will give you a copy of the tape," he laughed.

"They film it?"

"Sure. Everyone knows that."

I didn't fuckin' know that.

Now that he mentioned it, it might be a great dirty video to watch later on.

Ferdie stood. "You coming? There's been a staff changeover and a whole lot of cute new waiters."

I pushed my plate aside. "Studs with big dicks for you and twinks with cute asses for me."

Fuck, were they ever cute. I started on them as soon as I saw one to my liking. I took a few more pills but they weren't working like they should. My energy was flagging, my dick was limp. At this rate I was going to need something stronger in order to keep up. I found Ferdie sucking on some muscle dude's meat. I didn't wait for him to finish, just pulled him off and dragged him to a private corner to talk.

"What the fuck is the matter with you?" he screamed.

"Look," I said.

He looked at me as if I was mental. "What?"

I pointed at my cock which was as limp as a weathergirl's hair.

So help me, if the fucker laughed…

"What do you want me to do about it?" he asked.

"That stuff Morrie was talking about…"

"Maurice."

"Not you, too. Okay, Maurice. That shit he was talking about that makes you insatiable?"

"It really does make you insatiable. You keeping going until you're totally satisfied. I've seen some guys try to fuck themselves to death."

"Show me the way," I said. Sounded like that drug and my dick were made for each other.

"You sure?" Ferdie asked, concern in his voice.

"Shit, if it's that good, I may have to get two lots."

"Okay," he said.

We went to the opposite end of the room to a half hidden door and went into what had all the appearances of a doctor's surgery. The male nurse asked what we required and I hesitated to say it.

"You're among friends here," he said, ogling my crotch.

He was a cute fuck so, "Is he…?" I asked Ferdie.

"Sunday's shift," the twink smiled.

"I'll definitely check you out then," I said smugly.

We went through the formality, answered questions about what I'd taken so far, my medical history and all sorts of other bullshit. I smiled, though, when he asked, "Cock size?"

"You ask everyone that?"

"Only the men I want to fuck me."

Ferdie looked at the ceiling in disgust.

I noticed a couple of uglies in the waiting room obviously there for much the same reason as me. They leered. Or maybe I was getting paranoid. Either way, they weren't getting their hands on my tackle. A few more came in. This doc must be making a fortune.

The doctor came out. "Shane?"

I signaled him and he came over. He had a syringe in his hand. I didn't think he'd be so open about it that it would be done in the waiting room in front of other 'patients.' What did I care as long as it kept my dick hard?

"You frightened of needles?" he asked.

"I'm not a baby, doc."

He used an alcohol wipe and pumped the shit into my arm. It didn't take long before a strange sort of lethargy came over me, my whole body wouldn't obey my brain. What shit was this? I couldn't even speak, my mouth refused to work and I slurred. I turned to Ferdie and he shoved me. I fell sideways but he grabbed me before I could fall off the chair. He was laughing. So were the other guys in the room.

"I'll fuckin' kill you." That's what my brain said, but what my mouth did was drool and make a few non-specific sounds.

Ferdie slapped me across the face but I felt nothing.

Somewhere in the haze I heard him call. "Hey, doc. It's time for Shane's booty bump."

I knew what that meant from prison. It's when a guy shoots the drug ice, crystal meth, into his asshole with a needle-free syringe. I tried to stand but my body felt like it was made of rubber. Ferdie called some of the ugly slugs over to help him and the doctor. I tried to resist but I couldn't co-ordinate my movements. They stripped me, bent me over a chair and pulled my ass cheeks apart. I saw the doc with the syringe but didn't feel anything as I assumed he shot the drug into my vulnerable ass. Next time I saw the syringe, it was empty.

Fuck, was I in trouble now.

My brain was screaming as I was bundled out of the room and back to the central play area. A few guys watched from various lounges as I was manhandled onto a divan, face down, my ass exposed. Someone produced a plastic bottle of lube and squeezed a dollop onto their fingers. I knew it was being greased all over my ass. All the men around me including the fat uglies took a turn lubing my butt and I knew they were taking great delight in fingering me. I woulda puked if I coulda.

I'd kill the whole fuckin' lot of them when the drug wore off.

Someone spun me over onto my back and I screamed inwardly as I saw the waiter who'd been stirring the drinks with his cock bearing down on me. Ferdie held one of my legs in the air and Maurice held the other making my ass totally available to the monster cock. He rubbed some of the grease into his cock then kneeled between my legs and pushed. I grimaced expecting it to hurt but I felt nothing. Not yet. He fucked me hard. Calling me names that seemed to rattle around in my head as if they came from miles away.

His sweat dripped onto my face as he sneered while his cock pounded my guts. I was being fucked hard by the biggest cock I had ever seen. He shuddered, pushed into me and remained there, obviously blowing his load inside me. The first time I'd got spunk in my ass. Pulling out he kneeled over my face to push his slimy prick in my mouth until my saliva had washed it clean. I tasted nothing.

Someone took over from Ferdie, holding my leg in place as my next-door neighbor stripped out of his trousers and aimed his cock at my ass.

"You should see your asshole now, Shane. Red raw, spunk dribbling out of your cunt lips. You'll get such a treat when you see it in close-up on the wide screen TV in the bar. I've wanted your cunt for so long you fuckin' bastard I'm just sorry you won't feel the full impact this time. But there'll be others."

He slammed into me, crushing my balls. That I felt. The first drug that seemed to paralyze me was wearing off. By the time Ferdie rode my ass for fifteen minutes or more, spitting in my face, cursing me in language that would have made even me blush, the first drug had almost worn off like the anesthetic you get at the dentist.

I could feel Ferdie's cock smashing its way into my sore ass. I felt my sphincter expand and contract as he pulled out only to slam back in again.

"By the time we've finished with you, you'll be begging me to fuck you. Begging all of us. Pleading with me to blow a load in your ass. Your ass will crave cock so badly you'll never get rid of the itch."

He blew and pulled out, wiping his cock on my cheek.

Maurice passed my leg to one of the uglies who surrounded me. They each took a turn, telling me what they wanted to do to my slut's body until all I could think of was how much I wanted their cocks in my ass and my mouth. When I found my voice, I pleaded, "Fuck my slutty ass, fill me with your ugly fuckin' cocks and your foul spunk. Fill my belly with your nut juice till I puke it up."

Their faces leered at me from between my upraised legs, their ugly sweaty bodies dripping onto my hot muscular bod. They were using me, treating me as a cum dump, unloading their nasty sperm deep inside me.

"Breed me, you ugly fuckers. Bang my ass till I bleed. Fill me with your slime until I'm drowning in it."

I passed in and out of consciousness, occasionally waking to find I was wrapped in a blanket alone. On those occasions I would cast off the covering and go searching out cock, riding any man I found, young, old, handsome, ugly, until I got what I wanted, their cum in my ass or my mouth.

My appetite for cock was voracious, I was never satisfied. I had to have more and more cock. I was cock crazy. Eventually I wandered downstairs from the VIP Room and began to molest the men dancing on the floor. They were only too happy to oblige and I was thrown to the floor as faces, cocks, asses, mouths, competed for my attention. I swallowed spunk down my throat and up my ass until I felt like I was one giant sperm slithering on the dance floor.

"Fuck me," I screamed before I passed out.

I heard voices in the background.

My eyes were too heavy to open so I just listened.

I heard Maurice's voice.

"Your plan worked, Ferdie. You should be well pleased."

"I finally got to fuck the arrogant cunt's ass."

"Five times. You must like it."

"I waited so long."

"Was it worth it?"

"What do you think?"

"I think it's time I tried it. There won't be much traction left but he seems to be a very popular addition to our stable."

"Once you train the smugness out of him."

I felt a cock near my asshole. It slid in easily but even so, it felt amazingly good. "Like fucking a plate of custard, Ferdie."

Maurice grunted a few times but came very quickly. He pulled out and I heard his zipper. "Still tight enough all things considered. Yes, I think we can find a spot for him on the staff. Of course, he'll be fucked senseless every weekend. The boys will make sure of that."

"I hope I'm around to see it," Ferdie laughed.

"What of his parents?"

"It was his dad sold him to me. Told me he and his wife never wanted to set eyes on the cunt again."

"No one will miss him?"

"His parole officer, but he'll give up eventually."

They both giggled at the little joke.

So that was their game. I'll kill the cunts.

I got ready to spring. I'd grab them both by the throat so quickly I'd crush the life out of them before they even…

My asshole itched.

Oh shit, no.

It itched some more. I knew there was only way to scratch that particular itch.

"Fuck me. Please," I begged.

Lydian Press

ABOUT THE AUTHOR

Barry Lowe writes about love and sex so he won't forget how to do it. When he's not scribbling his adventures for the Sydney gay weekly *SX*, or out doing field research, he's writing about love's wonderful variations for a series of smut eBooks, novels and anthologies for Lydian Press

Go to www.barrylowe.info

OTHER WORKS BY BARRY LOWE

Available in eBook and Print

PLAYS

THE DEATH OF PETER PAN: Gay Historical Romance

NOVELS & ANTHOLOGIES

BUSTING BILLY'S BUTT: A Gay Erotic Romance

Steve and Billy's monogamous relationship has gone stale until Billy, ever the exhibitionist, shows them a way to spice up their sex life.

THE MAJOR AND THE MINERS: A Gay Historical Romance

1930s Australia: Two men from opposite ends of the social spectrum. Is love enough to overcome the obstacles between them?

THE GRAVY TRAIN: A Murder Mystery with Recipes
Someone on the train has an appetite for murder!

A TOUCH OF THE SON: A Gay Novel
Their secret passion will lead them to hell. Will they be able to find their way back?

ROMANCING THE BONE: Gay Romance Erotica

OMG! NOT ANOTHER GAY EROTICA ANTHOLOGY?

ROUGH & READY: Gay Tough Guy Erotica

YOUR BOYFRIEND IS HOT: Gay Cuckold Erotica

BEAR SKIN: Hot Gay Bear Erotica

THE MORE THE MERRIER: Gay Gangbang Erotica

THE BOY IS A BOTTOM: Gay Anal Erotica

COCK-EYED OPTIMISTS: Gay Romance Erotica

BABY, I'M NOT A MONSTER: Gay Vampire and Other Paranormal Erotica

CHRISTMAS CRACKER: Gay Erotica for the Holidays

SELECTED SHORT FICTION

Available as eBooks

HOW MUCH IS THAT DOGGIE IN THE WINDOW

THE DAY OF THE CLIFFORDS

HE WON'T SEND ROSES

A RED ROSE BEFORE CRYING

PRIDE AND JOY

ROAD HUMP

THE GOOD, THE BAD, AND THE CUDDLY

THE GROOM CLOSET

TUNNEL VISION

HARD ON HIS HEELS

SPIN THE BOTTOM

THE NEW DAD'S CLUB

FOUR ON THE FLOOR

TAGGED BY THE TEAM

WANNA SHARE YOUR HUSBAND

For all Barry's titles please visit his page at:

lydianpress.com

Lydian Press is dedicated to bringing you the finest GLBTQ erotic literature on the web.

Visit us on the web at:

http://lydianpress.com